You Found Me

For my plans for you are plans of good and not evil, to give you the expected end.
Jeremiah 29:11

Taiwo Iredele Odubiyi

You Found Me

This is a work of fiction. The characters, incidents, and dialogues are products of the author's imagination and are not to be construed as real. Any resemblance to actual events or persons, living or dead, is entirely coincidental.

Copyright March 2010 by Taiwo Iredele Odubiyi
ISBN: 978-978-904-422-1

Published by:
Tender Heartslink,
Maryland, USA

WhatsApp: +1410-8187482
Website: www.pastortaiwoodubiyi.org
Facebook: Pastor (Mrs.) Taiwo Odubiyi,
            Pastor Taiwo Iredele Odubiyi's Novels &
Books,

Twitter: @pastortaiwoodub

Instagram: @pastortaiwoiredeleodubiyi

Praise for the books of Taiwo Iredele Odubiyi

"Like Taiwo Iredele Odubiyi's previous books, this work is more than just a novel. It is a manual on relationships ..."
    - Olukorede Yishau, The Nation Newspaper, Nigeria

"She carries her readers along throughout the beautifully woven plots. This consolidates Odubiyi's position as a leading Christian fiction writer ..."
    - Sunday Oguntola, The Nation Newspaper, Nigeria

"Good job! I have read all your books and WHAOO! I am speechless! ..."
    - Omolayooni, USA

" ... I desperately wished there were different words and phrases I could use but I found none. If I were Wole Soyinka, coining new uncharted words or phrases would have been a lot easier. My village-school background left me with very little knowledge of English vocabulary and I now feel bounded to using 'whaos!' 'incredible!' 'highly impressed!' to tell you how great this last work is! And so, I'd say **To Love Again** is a master-piece!"
    - Olabode Babatope, Lagos

"If you say **Love On The Pulpit** is a fictional work, I wouldn't argue but I would add that it's a Rhema. I read **Shadows From The Past** and it was also awesome. Thanks for touching my life through these books ..."
    - Ronke A, Lagos

"I have now finished reading **Oh Baby**! My reaction? Terrific! Unputdownable! …"

- Mrs. Kragha, Lagos

"I have just finished reading **In Love For Us**. I need the other books authored by you …"

- Kehinde, Dubai

"Your books are the best. And you know what? You are the bomb! …"

- Onyekachi, Lagos

"I have read **Oh Baby**! and like your previous books, I could not drop it until I have read it from cover to cover … I acknowledge it's a masterpiece. I am highly fascinated …"

- Pastor J.A. Adeniji, Lagos

"I have read six of your novels and I must say each novel carries a unique unction that gives tranquility to the heart of the reader. Inspirational is an understatement …"
- Ese, UK

"Your books are more than just a literature. Myself and my wife are once again blessed with the latest book …"
- Ayuba Barnabas Bindede, Abuja

"Your novels are soul lifting and highly inspiring."
- Bisi Ogunro

"I read **Tears on my Pillow** on Monday and got hooked! I got **To Love Again** during the week and finished

reading it within a day! I am hooked and seriously searching out for your other books! …"
- Joy

"Congrats. You have done it again! …"
                                    - Nike Fakorede, Lagos

"Since my wife and I read your books which we received during your first visit to KENYA with your husband, our lives have not been the same again in the area of relationship. The book **LOVE FEVER** is rich! …"
                                    - Pastor and Mrs. Eric, Kenya

"… We are so proud that you are a Nigerian … "
- Olaniyan Oluwadara

"I read your books **Tears On My Pillow**, **In Love For Us**, **Love On The Pulpit** and I felt God speaking to me through you …"
- Ngozi

"I've discovered that many youths who don't even like reading books cannot do without your novels. Also, I gave some copies of **Oh Baby**! to some married women … God has used the book to restore marriages."
- Foluke, Ibadan

Excerpts

… "Well, it's a normal thing, especially for a cool and handsome guy like you. In fact, people would think something was wrong should they discover that someone like you didn't have a girlfriend."

He chuckled. "Well, I'm sorry to disappoint you. I don't have a girlfriend and there's nothing wrong with me." …

… "I haven't met the right person." He said.

"What kind of a lady do you find attractive?" She asked, smiling.

He looked at her. Was she flirting with him? …

… Smiling, Ann said, "Tell me why I should marry you."

Sam laughed and put his spoon down. "Wow! That's a big question."

She laughed.

Even though he wasn't expecting the question, he began to talk. "You should marry me because I truly and sincerely love you …

… He shrugged. "Well, you can choose what you'll call me and I'll call you what I want. I prefer 'Baby'."

She smiled. "Okay. I prefer 'Mine'."

"Or better still, we can combine the two, and have 'Baby Mine'." …

Acknowledgment

As always, I'm starting by thanking God for His grace and all He has done for me. None of this would be possible without Him.

To my darling husband, Pastor Sola, *you've been there for me from day one. Thank you for your love, support and advice.*

To my children, *you're still my cheer-leaders. Thanks for all you do to encourage me.*

To my dear mother, Mrs. Victoria O. Soyombo, *you like reading my books! That means a lot to me. I know you still miss Daddy. I miss him too.*

To my dear brothers and sister, as well as their families, *thank you for always being there for me.*

To my loving parents-in-law, Mr. and Mrs. E.F. Odubiyi, *thank you, Daddy and Mommy, for your love and support.*

To my brother and sisters-in-law, *I appreciate your support.*

Wow! To the editors, Babatope Olabode, Pastor Sola Odubiyi, Edicheck.com, Biyi Fashoyin and Kola Kuforiji, *this book is much better because of you. Thanks.*

To Wole Dada and Tola Babatunde, *you make the front cover beautiful with your faces. Thanks for believing in my works.*

Thanks to all the people who kept asking me, 'When will another book be ready?' *That kept me going, and here it is. I appreciate you.*

To the people who have all my books, encourage and pray for me, *thanks sooooo much!*

And to all of my readers everywhere, *I love you and I look forward to hearing from you if this story has touched your heart.*

It's all about You! Pastor Taiwo Iredele Odubiyi

Dedication

To God,
And
to every man and woman looking for true love

 # Chapter 1

As Sam Jacobs was driving his boss's black 7-series BMW car toward Murtala Muhammed International Airport that Wednesday morning, with the windows up and the air conditioner on, he thought of where he could get a piece of cardboard to buy. His boss, Mr. Layi Noah who was the Managing Director of Best Insurance Company, had told him the previous week that he would be going to the airport to pick his niece, Ann, who was arriving from South Africa.

Just before Sam left Mr. Noah's house, the man wrote his niece's name on a small piece of paper and gave it to Sam, instructing him to get the cardboard on his way. He explained that it would be better to write her name out in bold lettering on cardboard which Sam would hold out for her to see, for easy identification since he didn't know her in person.

There were many stores at the airport, but Sam wasn't certain any of them would have cardboards. He looked at the time on the dashboard. It was 7.50am. He still had time. The traffic was light today and Ann's plane was due to arrive at 9.20am.

It occurred to him to go to a particular store that was on the way to the airport, although he would have to turn off the airport road a little, but he was certain he would get cardboard there. He decided to go to the store and soon, he was parking in front of Kaybee Store. He turned the air conditioner and engine off, locked up the car and walked briskly into the big store. It didn't take him long to find what he wanted. He took a white cardboard, got a red marker as well, and paid.

As he walked back to the car, he could hear some birds singing as the morning sun announced its majestic appearance.

Inside the car, he took the marker and wrote the lady's name on the cardboard in bold letters: ANN LOLA SANKEY.

He looked at it and nodded. It was legible enough. Placing the cardboard on the passenger seat, he started the car, turned the air conditioner on, and joined the flow of traffic again, on his way to the airport. He glanced briefly at the shrubs that adorned the express road and thought they were beautiful.

He inserted a CD of Maurette Brown Clark. As the CD played, he sang along.

Just want to praise You,
Forever and ever, and ever,
For all You've done for me ...

He got to the airport at 8.20am. Paying the toll, he drove into the parking lot and parked. He took the cardboard, folded it, stepped out of the car and locked up.

There were many people in front of the arrival hall.

Sam stood on a side, wondering where he could sit while he awaited the arrival of Ann's flight. Then, he decided to get something to eat as he had not eaten. He left and entered another hall, looking around. He saw a restaurant, bureau de change, and a bank.

He went to the restaurant. There, he bought club sandwiches and a cup of tea. Making himself comfortable on one of the tall seats, he began to eat, and at the same time, send text messages to the executive members of *Agape Campus Church* in *Livingston University*, to remind them of the meeting they would have on Sunday, after service.

From where he sat, he could hear a female voice announcing flight departures and arrivals.

****

As Ann returned from the restroom, she heard the announcement that the plane would be landing shortly. The flight attendants began to move around, telling passengers to use their seatbelts and ensure their seatbacks were up and the tray tables were in locked positions.

"Excuse me please." Ann told the middle-aged woman on the aisle seat.

The woman moved her legs to a side, to allow Ann pass to her window seat. Ann did, sat down and pulled the seatbelt round her waist. Bringing out her make-up purse, she quickly renewed her makeup. She took her hairbrush, brushed her weave-on hair backward, and sprayed some perfume. When she was through, she began to look out of the window by her side.

Soon, she could see houses and vehicles. They were now in Nigeria. Wondering if the country would have changed in any way since she travelled out three years ago, she hoped she would not regret coming back.

She really liked South Africa and wanted to live permanently there. Two of her friends in High School lived there and they had been asking her to come over. She had begun to think about it. And when she graduated from University, she told her parents of her desire to travel and they gave their consent. She travelled to stay with her friend in Pretoria and found out that her friend was living with a man. Ann didn't like that and had moved to Johannesburg two months after, to stay with the second friend.

But about two months ago, her mother's only sibling, Mr. Layi Noah told her it would be better she returned to Nigeria, adding that quite a number of people who had travelled abroad were coming back home and were better off. He had promised to help her get a good job and when two weeks after, he'd called back to say he had a job waiting for her, she had agreed to return. If things didn't turn out well for her, she could always travel out again after all, she had her legal resident permit already.

It would be nice to see her parents again anyway. Her fifty six-year old mother had been ill some time ago. Everyone had been worried, thinking she would die but she had recovered. Three of her siblings were in different countries and only her younger brother lived with her parents. She would not be able to stay with her parents though because it would be too far to *First Place Investment Company*, where she would work. She would have to live with Mr. Noah's family as she had already told him, being aware that only Olu, their third child lived with them. Their firstborn, twenty six-year old Ola, lived in France, and Nike, who was two months younger than Ann had travelled to Ukraine.

Ann was certain Mr. Noah and his wife would not mind her staying with them. He had been a true brother to her mother. He and his wife had been very nice to her family, and her family was close to them.

Soon, the wheels of the plane touched ground and most of the passengers clapped for the safe landing.

****

"Attention please."

Sam heard the announcement over the public address system that the South African flight had arrived. He looked at his watch. The time was 8.55am. The flight was early. He was glad he came on time. He quickly finished his drink, took the cardboard and got up. He went to stand with the crowd in front of the arrival hall.

About twenty minutes later, the passengers on the flight began to come out. He held up the cardboard when he saw a young lady approaching, but an elderly couple from the crowd called her and she went to them. As more people came out, Sam kept the cardboard up, hoping he would get Ann easily.

From the way Mr. Noah had spoken about Ann, Sam assumed she would be between twenty and twenty six years of age. Mr. Noah had also said she was light in complexion.

Sam concentrated on light-complexioned young ladies. If he saw one approaching, he would hold the cardboard up in her direction, for her to see.

A fair, young lady who limped approached, pushing her cart. She was looking at the cardboards people held up.

Could it be Ann? Sam wondered. But Mr. Noah hadn't told him she limped, he thought as he kept the cardboard up.

The lady looked at it and walked past him. It wasn't Ann.

Another approached, scanning the faces of the people standing. Sam saw her look in his direction. Ann? The lady suddenly squealed with delight, left her luggage cart and raced toward him. Wondering at the show of emotion from a stranger, he plastered a smile on his face and waited for her to come but she ran past him into the arms of a thin man beside him.

So, where's Ann? What's keeping her? He wondered. More than fifty passengers had come out and many of the people he was standing with had left, having seen the persons they were waiting for.

****

Pulling her hand luggage behind her, Ann cleared the immigration section and followed the other passengers to the luggage claim area. She looked around and saw some luggage carts arranged in a corner. Walking over, she tried to pull one.

"Hey, Madam!" Someone shouted from behind her.

She stopped and looked back. A man in green uniform came to her.

"You have to pay one hundred naira!" The man said.

"Oh, okay." She said. "I don't have naira notes though. Do you accept dollars?"

"Yes."

"How much for a cart?"

"One dollar."

Opening her purse, she brought a dollar bill out. "Here, take."

"Go there and pay." The man said roughly, pointing in another direction.

Taking a breath to calm down, Ann left for the other place. As she awaited her turn to pay for a cart, she removed her jacket. The weather was very hot. She looked around and saw some of the other passengers also holding their jackets in their hands while some had theirs tied round their waists. If she had had any doubt of being back in Nigeria, it was now gone. *This is indeed Nigeria!*

Soon, she paid, got a receipt and went back to where the other man was, giving him the receipt of payment. He perforated it, gave it back to her and pulled a cart out. Dropping her hand luggage on the cart, she pushed it to the carousel and stood with other passengers. People were making calls on their cell phones to inform their families and friends of their arrival. She didn't have a phone she could use. She could only hope that Sam, the driver her uncle said would pick her up would be waiting for her so she wouldn't have to stay long at the airport. If she didn't see him though, she might have to look for a phone to use to call her uncle.

Soon, one of her three suitcases came out and she put it on the cart. Shortly after, another one came out and she took it. It remained one. When she had not seen the third suitcase ten minutes after, she began to worry. Could something have happened to it? She asked one of the men standing beside her.

The man shook his head. "I don't think so. They don't tamper with bags here. You'll soon see it as bags are still coming out."

Suddenly, she spotted it coming.

"Oh, there it is!" She said and let out a sigh of relief.

The man laughed. "I told you."

She got it, put it on the cart as well and left, pushing the cart.

When she emerged outside the arrival hall with the cart, she saw many people. Some were holding white papers and cardboards on which names were written. As she made her way forward slowly, a fair-skinned young man approached her.

"Beautiful girl, do you need a cab?"

Tightening her grip on her purse which contained her international passport, Ann shook her head to decline.

"Hey, Madam, do you need help?" Another man asked her.

"No." Ann answered.

She hadn't remembered to ask her uncle how she would identify the driver he said would pick her.

She scanned the crowd. The driver should be a middle-aged man and most likely dark in complexion. He might also have facial marks, she thought. With this in mind, she began to move slowly; looking at the names written on the papers and cardboards, and also looking at people whom she thought might be drivers. She looked at them closely and a little longer than necessary, in case one of them would recognize her or call her name.

Still pushing the cart forward slowly, she saw a man who seemed to match her description. He wore a brown uniform, and held a cardboard. She squinted her eyes to read the name on the paper. It was Hauwa Baba.

Ann continued to walk down slowly, hoping she wouldn't have a hard time getting the driver.

Suddenly, she saw her name! She stopped to look at the name on the cardboard again. It was her name, no doubt.

She looked at the person holding it. The dark, tall man was nothing like she had expected. He was a young man, in his twenties and handsome. He wore a white T-shirt on a pair of blue jeans, and white snickers. Then the man looked at her and she raised her left hand slightly in greeting.

****

Sam saw two young ladies coming. One of them was light in complexion and they seemed to be looking for someone. He raised the name-cardboard in their direction. As they walked past him, he thought one of them looked familiar. Was she an actress or a singer? He wasn't sure of where he'd seen the face before.

He looked away from them and found another light-complexioned slender lady, of an average height, looking directly at him!

She wore a light pink blouse that had a plunging neckline on deep pink trousers, and held in her right hand a jacket which matched the trousers. Her hair was long. Her left hand which was resting on the handle of the cart had two rings, one on the index finger and the other on the middle finger. Could it be Ann? Would she come in his direction?

She raised her left hand slightly, then began to push her cart in his direction.

She must be the one. Sam moved immediately and went to her.

"Hello. Are you Ann Lola Sankey?" He asked, his eyes going to her lips that shimmered with pink lipstick and gloss.

"Yes."

"Mr. Noah asked me to pick you up."

"Thank you. Are you Sam?" She expected him to say no.

He nodded and smiled broadly, "Yes. You're welcome back to Nigeria." He shook hands with her.

"Thank you."

"I'll help you with that." He said.

"Thank you." She repeated and stepped back.

Sam took the handle of the cart. "Let's go. The car is at the parking lot."

"Okay."

Then he looked down at her shoes. The open-toe pink shoes were very high. He also noticed that her toenails were painted pink.

"Er … can you walk far with your shoes or would you rather wait somewhere, for me to bring the car?" He asked.

She shrugged. "My shoes are not a problem."

He pushed the cart away from where people were and stopped.

Taking his phone, he pressed some buttons. "Hello sir - yes - yes - she's here with me. Hold on for her."

He held the phone out to Ann, "Your uncle."

She took it and soon began to talk and laugh. Looking at her, Sam noticed her well-manicured nails and thought, *she's beautiful and elegant.*

When she was through, she returned the phone to him. "Thank you."

He began to push the cart and she walked beside him.

"How was the flight?"

"Oh, I guess it was okay. Thanks."

"How many hours was it?"

"About six hours." She told him.

After walking a little distance, he told her to wait with the cart.

"The park is still a little distance from here. I'll bring the car to you."

"Okay, thanks."

He left and briskly walked to the park. About eight minutes after, he got to where she was standing and flashed the lights at her.

She peeped and recognized him behind the wheel.

Sam parked the car and got down, loading her suitcases into the boot of the car.

Ann entered the passenger seat and fastened the seatbelt. Soon they were on their way.

"Please, could I use your phone briefly? I need to call my parents."

He gave his phone to her. Once again, he heard her laughing as she talked.

As she returned the phone some minutes later, she asked, "Will my uncle be at home?"

"No, he's at work."

"Okay."

She turned to look out the window and began to talk about her observations as Sam sped on.

When she stopped talking, he asked, "How is South Africa?"

She turned to look at him. "SA is an interesting place. It's a place you should go."

Sam smiled, "Some of my friends have told me that."

"Oh, your friends? Where do they live in SA?"

"Some of them are in Pretoria."

"Well, if you go to SA, they should take you to Menlyn Mall, Sandton City Mall, Eastgate Mall."

As she continued to mention the names of places of interest in Pretoria, Sam exclaimed, "Wow!"

"And if you happen to be in Johannesburg, one of the places you should visit is Montecasino."

She proceeded to tell him about the place.

"It appears you have fallen in love with the country."

She laughed. "Maybe. I hope I will be able to cope with life in Nigeria again."

"You were born here, weren't you?"

"Yes." She answered.

"By the way, why have you returned?"

"My uncle encouraged me to come back." She said.

"When was your last time in Nigeria?"

"I travelled three years ago, after I graduated from university."

He was surprised. "You graduated three years ago?" He looked sideways at her briefly.

She nodded.

"Wow! That's great. You look very young."

"Not so young though. I'm twenty four, well … almost twenty four."

He laughed a little, "When will you be twenty four?"

"In about five months."

Hmm, that meant he was nine months older than her. She had graduated three years ago while he was still in university, he thought and smiled.

He didn't allow such thoughts to bother him though. It wasn't as if it was his fault he was still in school. He was not a dullard. He didn't need anyone to tell him he was intelligent, he knew he was. He had finished from High School at the age of sixteen with very good grades but knowing his parents were not rich and would not be able to afford University fees, he had decided to work for a while. He had gotten a job as a clerk in a company where one of his father's friends worked and he was there for two years. While there, he got one of the staff to teach him to drive. At eighteen, he got admission as a part-time student in Livingston University and two years after, changed his job to become Mr. Noah's driver as the salary was a little higher.

Slowing down to negotiate a bend, he said, "Wow! That's interesting."

"Do you work for my uncle?" Ann asked.

"Yes."

"As his driver?"

"Yes."

"But … you can do better than that, don't you think? You're a young guy and I think you're smart. Why don't you try to further your studies?"

He laughed a little. "I'm in my final year in Livingston University."

"Oh, really? You work and go to school?"

"Yes, I have to."

"People do it. Well, that's smart and good. I thought as much, you don't seem like a regular driver."

He laughed. "I guess I should say 'Thank you'."

She laughed. "What are you studying?"

"Estate Management."

"Did my uncle tell you someone is arriving from SA tomorrow as well?"

He shook his head. "No, he didn't."

"Well … he knows about it. I will remind him when I get to the house. But could you bring me tomorrow evening to pick the person?"

"Yes I can, as soon as your uncle gives me the order. I work for him."

"Could I use your phone to call him?"

"Yes, you can but why don't you wait till you get to the house?"

"I may forget by then. Since we are talking about it now, I think I should just discuss it with him. It will enable you plan your program as well."

Smiling, he dialed Mr. Noah's number and gave her the phone.

"Uncle, it's me, Ann. I told you Daniel will arrive tomorrow. Who will take me to the airport to meet him? - oh Sam? - the flight is arriving at 7.30pm - okay, thank you, Uncle."

She ended the call and gave the phone to Sam.

"He obviously forgot to mention it to you. He said you will take me to the airport."

"That's okay." Sam said.

"Thank you."

"Is Daniel your brother?" He asked.

"No, he's my boyfriend."

"Oh, I see. Is he coming from SA as well?"

"Yes."

"Is he a Nigerian?"

She smiled. "Yes."

"Coming back finally?"

"Well, he has not really decided but he will be around for a while."

"For how long are you going to be in Nigeria?"

She shrugged. "I don't know. For as long as I have to, I guess. I will be resuming in an office soon though."

"Where's that?"

She told him.

Soon, they arrived at Mr. Noah's house. The house was a detached bungalow with a large compound. It had a high fence and a shop that opened to the street which Mrs. Noah managed, selling soft drinks and groceries. It also had a double garage and a rear garden.

Seeing that Mrs. Noah's shop was open, Sam pressed the horn twice. A young lady emerged from the shop and told him that Olu would open the gate.

"Thank you." He told the lady.

The gate was opened by Olu and Sam drove into the compound, parking beside Mrs. Noah's white Toyota Liteace bus.

Leaving her female staff, Mrs. Funke Noah came out of the shop through the back door. The plump woman wore a long skirt and blouse, and her hair was wrapped in a black scarf.

She greeted Ann warmly, hugging her. Olu, who was nineteen years old, also greeted Ann.

Sam brought the three suitcases out of the car. Olu pulled one while Sam pulled the other two.

"Let me pull this." Ann told Sam, reaching out for one of the suitcases.

"Don't worry." He said.

"Thanks."

Ann took her hand luggage and following Mrs. Noah, they entered the house through the entrance hall. The wall was painted white and the floor was tiled.

"You're going to stay in Nike's room." Mrs. Noah informed Ann.

Ann knew the room as she had stayed there with Nike a number of times when they were both in High School.

"That's okay. Thank you, Aunty."

They walked past the living room, kitchen, master bedroom, and visitor's toilet.

Then Mrs. Noah opened a door and they entered. Ann looked around. The room looked the same, only Nike's personal things were no longer there. The cream-colored room with a matching carpet had a built-in closet and a white ceiling fan. A well laid, queen-size bed with two pillows was on a side of the room with some space between it and the wall. A small table on which was a lamp with a blue shade was by the bed, against the wall.

The shade had tassels round the end. There was also a dresser with a mirror. A clock and a painting hung on the wall. On the right was the door of the adjoining bathroom.

"Thank you, Aunty." Ann repeated. She sat on the bed and removed her shoes.

Sam pulled the three suitcases to the front of the closet. He made to leave the room, turned and asked Ann, "What time do you want me to get here tomorrow to pick you up?"

"I don't know. What time do you think we should leave, taking the traffic situation into consideration?"

"I'll be here by 5.30pm."

"I guess that's okay. Thanks for everything." She told him.

"I'm leaving." Sam told Mrs. Noah.

"Okay. Thanks for your help."

Ann, Mrs. Noah and Olu went to the living room. The room was cool, and Ann knew the air conditioner must be working. She looked round the room which had white ceiling. Paintings and enlarged family pictures adorned the beige wall of the exquisitely furnished large room. A large flatscreen TV was in a corner and beside it was a table on which were magazines.

There was a door on the far left which Ann knew led to the balcony. She stood up, went there and opened the door. She stepped on the balcony where there were a recliner, four cane-chairs with cushions, and a table with an oak top.

Ann returned to the living room and sat. She began to ask about other members of the Noah family and friends.

"Do you and Nike get in touch with each other?" Mrs. Noah asked.

"Yes, regularly. We also communicate on Facebook and Twitters."

They continued talking.

Eventually Mrs. Noah got up.

"I've prepared food for you. It's spaghetti with shredded beef in pepper sauce."

"Wow!" Ann exclaimed and laughed. "That sounds nice."

Smiling, Mrs. Noah continued, "You may want to shower and freshen up before eating though."

"I have to. The weather is very hot! How do you cope?"

"How were you coping before you left for SA?"

"Honestly, I can't remember."

They laughed.

Ann got up and returned to the bedroom. Opening the three suitcases, she took the things she would need and entered the adjoining bathroom.

About twenty minutes after, she reappeared in the living room, wearing a short-sleeved cotton shirt on a pair of jeans.

Mrs. Noah was still there but her son had left. As Ann ate, they talked.

Mrs. Noah's cell phone began to ring. "It's my husband." She said to Ann before picking the call. "Hello."

She talked with him for some minutes before giving the phone to Ann.

When the call ended, Mrs. Noah told Ann, "If you need to make calls, you can use the house phone. It's in that corner." She pointed to a table in a far corner.

"Okay. Thank you, Aunty."

Ann finished eating and washed her plates in the kitchen. The white room had a big refrigerator, deep freezer, gas cooker with oven, stainless steel sink, a plate rack, a table with marble top, shelves, as well as cabinets. A waste basket was on a side by one of the cabinets.

She returned to the living room and began to use the cordless phone to make calls. She called her parents and brother, Biodun. She also called some of her friends.

Afterward, she returned to her room. Opening her luggage, she brought out the gifts she had bought for her uncle's family, putting them on the bed. She was getting out the gifts for her parents when there was a brief knock on the door.

"Yes, come in."

The door opened to reveal Mrs. Noah.

"I'll be going to the salon to fix my hair soon."

"Can I come with you?" Ann asked.

"Sure, if you want to but I thought you would be tired."

"I'm not. Please, give me a few minutes. I'll join you."

Closing the suitcases on the floor, Ann brought out a pair of black sandals from her hand luggage and wore them.

Soon, they left the house and walked to the salon which was at the end of the long street.

Not long after they returned at 5.30pm, Mr. Noah arrived. The tall, large man was obviously happy to see his favorite niece, as he gave her a big hug.

"It's good to see you again." Ann told him.

They sat and began to discuss generally. Later, Ann went to her room to bring the gifts she had for the couple and their son, and gave them.

At about 8pm, she retired into her room, had a shower and changed into her nightwear. Taking her small Bible from her hand luggage, she opened it to Psalm 27 and put it under her pillow as she had been doing for about six months.

She had been seeing her late paternal grandmother in her dreams. And sometimes, she saw her late paternal grandfather as well. And this happened at least twice in a month. When she told one of her friends in South Africa, the friend had advised her to get a Bible, open it to Psalm 27 and put it under her pillow whenever she wanted to sleep. She had bought a small Bible and had been putting it under her pillow even if it was just a nap, yet the dreams had not stopped. She didn't know what else to do.

Although her parents were not regular church-goers, they were not the type to go to spiritualists or witch-doctors. At times like this, she wished they were. She had told her mother on phone about the dreams, but her mother hadn't suggested any solution. She had simply told her not to worry, and that the dreams would stop with time. Ann hoped her mother was right.

Ann slept and saw both of her late grandparents in her dream again. Suddenly waking up, she wondered what to do. She took the Bible from under her pillow and opened to Psalm 91 which another person had suggested to her, reading it twice.

She returned the Bible under her pillow and slept back. This time, she saw one of her classmates in Elementary School, swimming in a river. The girl whom she hadn't seen since she graduated from the school beckoned at her. Ann shook her head and remained at the edge of the river, looking at the girl. Suddenly, the girl pulled her hand, trying to draw her into the river. Ann resisted. As she struggled with the girl, she tried to wake up from the bad dream but couldn't. She tried to open her mouth to talk or call someone for help but couldn't. She tried to move her hands and feet, but this too seemed impossible as she felt tied down. After a lot of struggle, she woke up, sweating. When would these dreams stop?

She glanced at the wall clock. The time was 4.13am. She was scared of going back to sleep but what else could she do at this time of the day? She eventually slept back.

She woke up at about 8am. Wearing a pink robe over her nightwear, she left the room and went to the living room. Mr. Noah was standing, talking with his wife. Sam stood behind him, with Mr. Noah's briefcase in his hand.

She greeted the couple and Sam, before sitting down. Her eyes went to Sam. He was in jeans again, but this time, he wore a white cotton shirt and dark blue snickers.

Suddenly, he looked in her direction and their eyes met.

Ann looked away.

Mr. Noah called her, "Sam will come in the evening to take you to the airport."

"Okay. Thank you, Uncle."

Soon, Mr. Noah and Sam left.

Back in her room, Ann began to unpack, hanging her clothes in the closet.

After having her bath and breakfast, she called one of her friends to come and take her out. The friend did and brought her back at about 4pm.

 # Chapter 2

At 5.14pm, Sam arrived. Ann was ready but was watching a soap opera on TV.

"Please, I want to watch this to the end. It's ending at 5.30pm."

She and Mrs. Noah laughed.

Smiling, Sam glanced at his watch.

She noticed it and said, "Pleeeease!"

He laughed a little. "That's fine. I'll be in the car."

In the car, he inserted a musical CD.

At 5.34pm, he saw Ann walking toward the car. She wore a red dress that was low in upper front and had a thigh-revealing slit on the lower side. Sam didn't like the dress as it revealed her cleavage and thigh. But considering her color combination, face and hair, he had to admit she was a beautiful lady.

He reached out and opened the passenger door for her.

She entered and the car was immediately filled with the scent from her perfume. *That's a nice one*, he thought as he greeted her.

"Hi." She said, hooking her seatbelt.

"Hi." He responded, noticing the two rings on her left hand.

Relaxing on her seat, she opened her purse, took her gold tinted sunglasses and wore it.

As Sam pulled out and joined the traffic, he began to talk with her.

"That's a good perfume you're wearing." He commented.

"Thank you." She said and smiled, revealing her well set teeth.

"And you look good as well but I'm sure I'm not the first person to tell you this." He said, a little smile tugging at the corners of his mouth.

She smiled again. "What if I said you're the first person?"

"I would not believe it. Your boyfriend must have told you several times."

She laughed, "Yes, he has."

He liked the way she laughed. He stopped the CD that was playing.

Smiling, he told her, "And many other men must have said so."

She laughed again.

"But I believe you will radiate more beauty and be a better person if well … you'll have a good relationship with God. Or do you?" He took his eyes off the road briefly to look at her.

"What do you mean?" She asked with a frown.

"I'm just wondering if you are a church person." He said and smiled.

"Well, it depends on what you mean."

He smiled. "I mean, do you have a personal relationship with God? … although, I already have my answer."

"Well, er …"

He smiled again. "Were you attending any church in SA?"

She looked at him and thought, *oh, he's one of those people who take Christianity very serious*. Before she left the country for SA, one of her female course mates had talked to her about God, telling her she had to be born again, whatever that meant. She'd had to tell the lady to stop coming.

Thinking of how to respond to Sam's question, she began, "Well, er -"

Still smiling, Sam began to talk to her about God.

His style and approach seemed different from that lady's, Ann thought, and found herself listening to him.

Some minutes after, he asked, "Would you like to pray now?"

She agreed, prayed and gave her life to Jesus, to Sam's surprise and delight.

"Do you have a Bible?"

"Yes. I have a small one." She told him.

"Does it contain both old and new testaments?"

"Yes."

"That's fine. You will need to read it so that you can know your rights as a child of God. You can start from the Gospel of John. Try to read a chapter per day. You will also need to pray regularly … and find a living church to worship. I know your uncle's family doesn't go regularly."

"Which church do you attend?" She asked.

"Agape Campus Church."

She had never heard of it. "Where is it?"

"It's a fellowship on my campus." He told her.

They continued talking until they reached the airport.

He stopped for her in front of the arrival hall. "You can get down. I'll go and park the car, and meet you here."

"No, it's okay. My sandals don't have very high heels. You can continue to the parking lot. We'll walk back together to the arrival hall."

He proceeded to the parking lot where he parked the car and they got down. Side by side, they walked to the arrival hall, talking.

Sam felt a little self-conscious. If students who knew him to be the Vice President of Agape Campus Church should see him with Ann with the way she was dressed, what would they think?

In front of the arrival hall, Ann looked around. It seemed busier than it was yesterday when she arrived.

They were early, so they stood on a side. As they talked, Sam kept his eyes on her face, away from her cleavage. He noticed her well-shaped brows and long eyelashes.

A flight had just arrived from New York and passengers were coming out.

Unaware of Sam's uneasiness, Ann continued talking. "So, do you have a girlfriend?" She asked, smiling.

Surprised, he laughed, then looked at her for several seconds before he asked, "Why did you ask?"

Laughing, she shrugged, "It's just a question."

Still laughing, he said, "Well … no."

She looked surprised. "Why not?"

He laughed again. "Must I?"

"Well, it's a normal thing, especially for a cool and handsome guy like you. In fact, people would think something was wrong should they discover that someone like you didn't have a girlfriend."

He chuckled. "Well, I'm sorry to disappoint you. I don't have a girlfriend and there's nothing wrong with me."

"That's strange." Her gaze studied his face.

"It's not. Besides, these things are a little different for Christians. They have to pray first, to be sure of who the right person is. Then they go into dating, then courtship, followed by engagement, and then marriage. So, it's not really a case of girlfriend and boyfriend. It's much more than that."

"Oh, I see." She said, even though she didn't see anything. Why must they pray? Was love not all that mattered? And what did he mean by *It's not really a case of girlfriend and boyfriend?*

She asked another question. "Have you ever been in a relationship?"

He laughed again. "May I know why you're asking me all these questions?"

"I'm just trying to get to know you better." She replied and laughed. "I will answer whatever question you ask me, when it's your turn."

"When it's my turn?" He asked. *What kind of a person is she?* He wondered and laughed.

"Am I having my turn?" He asked.

"Well, that's what I said." She said and laughed.

"That's funny."

"You haven't answered my question." She reminded him.

"What question? Oh, if I've ever had a relationship?"

"Yes."

Smiling, he said, "Well, I was interested in a girl at a time. That was about five years ago, before I became a Christian."

"Before you became a Christian?"

He nodded.

"How old were you then?"

"I was nineteen."

She did a quick mental calculation and said, "So, you're about the same age as me."

"Yes."

"Which month is yours?"

"March."

"Hmm. How old was the girl then?"

He closed his eyes briefly as he tried to remember, "I think she was also nineteen."

"So, what happened after you became a Christian?"

"My priorities changed. I had to end the relationship. Besides, at the age of nineteen, what did we know about relationship? I'm glad I knew the truth on time before I got into trouble."

"How did the girl take the breakup?"

Sam didn't like these questions about his personal life and had the mind to tell her so. But ... she had just given her life to God. It could be that she was trying to know some things about relationships. He shouldn't discourage her.

"Well, I'm sure she didn't like it but it had to be done. It was the right thing for me to do."

"Have you seen her since then?"

"I attended a wedding at a time and saw her."

"Wow!" She smiled. "That's interesting."

They didn't talk for about a minute.

She spoke again, "Since Christians have to pray about relationship, why don't you have someone you are praying about?"

"I haven't met the right person." He said.

"What kind of a lady do you find attractive?" She asked, smiling.

He looked at her. Was she flirting with him?

With a corner of his mouth turning up in a smile, he asked, "What exactly are you driving at? Why are you asking me these questions? What do you want to know about me?"

She laughed.

"It's my turn to ask questions." He said.

She laughed again and told him, "Go ahead."

"What I'd like to know is if you're always this direct."

She laughed. "Well, I like to say what's on my mind."

"Even where men are concerned?"

"As I said earlier, I just wanted to get to know you better."

"So you said, and I understand. Er ... can I be as direct as you have been?"

As she nodded, she had a feeling she wasn't going to like what he would say.

"I find the questions rather funny. Another man might take them the wrong way though. He might think you're trying to patronize him."

"I understand what you're saying. I wasn't doing any such thing though. I have a boyfriend and I'm not complaining, thank you." She laughed again.

Thank you? He laughed.

"Is Daniel your only boyfriend?" The question had popped out of his mouth before he realized it wasn't the right question.

She looked at him sharply. "Of course. That's a funny question. Do I look like someone who would have more than one guy?"

He smiled to show he didn't mean to insult her. "Well, like you, I am only trying to get to know you better." He said carefully.

He could have asked about Daniel, but he didn't really want to know about her love life. *Only God knows what she has been doing with the boyfriend*, he thought. She had just given her life to God, but the significance obviously hadn't dawned on her. Not certain how to handle her, he took a deep breath.

"How many siblings do you have?"

She told him.

She suddenly changed the line of discussion and said, "I'm thirsty. Can I get something to drink?"

"Oh, sure."

Glancing briefly at his watch, he said, "We still have some time. Let's go."

They went to the restaurant inside. Sam pulled out one of the seats for her and sat on one himself.

"What will you like to drink?"

"I'll take juice." Then opening her purse, she added, "I have some money here."

"I'll take care of it." Sam said, smiling broadly.

"Thanks."

He ordered two cans of juice and as they sipped, they talked.

Then he said, "Is there anything you will want me to pray about with you?"

She told him about the dreams she had been having and the ones she had last night. She also told him that she had been placing her Bible under her pillow, opening it to different Psalms. As she talked, he listened intently.

He told her, "Opening to different chapters of the book of Psalms and putting it under your pillow does not mean much. It is the contents of the Bible which you know in your heart and act on, that will make the dreams stop. Now that you are a Christian, you should simply pray and cancel such dreams. You have authority as a Christian and your word contains power. Many Scriptures talk about the Christian's authority. A verse says you shall decree a thing and it shall be established to you."

"Is that in the Bible?" Ann asked.

"Yes."

She had never seen it before. "Where is it in the Bible?"

"It's in the book of Job. I have a Bible in the car. I'll show you later."

They continued talking.

Soon, they heard the announcement of the arrival of the flight.

"Oh, it's here." She said with excitement.

They finished their drinks and left.

The passengers began to come out, pushing carts. Ann kept a close watch at the exit door.

Suddenly she said, "That's him!"

Sam looked and saw a light-skinned man who could be a little older than him. He was dressed in suit.

Ann left Sam's side and went to Daniel, hugging him. Sam followed and stood quietly behind her.

She introduced them, "Daniel, this is Sam." She gestured toward Sam. "He brought me." And turning to Sam, she said, "Sam, this is Daniel."

Sam shook hands with Daniel, giving a polite smile.

Daniel thanked him for coming to pick him.

"The car is outside at the park." Sam said.

He didn't offer to push the luggage cart for Daniel but simply walked behind them. He could see that the two of them were happy to see each other. He hoped Ann would stand as a Christian. Well, he had done what he had to do, the rest was God's part, he thought.

When they got to a spot, he asked them to wait while he went to the parking lot to bring the car. He soon brought the car to them. Daniel had a possessive arm around Ann. Sam assisted Daniel to put his two suitcases in the boot.

Ann asked Daniel, "Will you sit in front with Sam?"

"No." Daniel said without hesitation. "I'll prefer to sit at the back with you. I've missed you." He slid his arm around her waist, pulled her close and kissed her briefly.

Sam looked away and entered the car while Daniel got into the back seat with Ann.

"Where are we going?" Sam asked.

"Oh, I'm sorry." Daniel said. "We are going to Casper Estate. Do you know how to get there?"

"Yes." Sam answered. It was a neighborhood of the rich. He had driven Mr. Noah to the estate a number of times.

As Sam drove on, Ann and Daniel talked in low tones and sometimes he heard Ann's chuckle and sounds that suggested they were kissing. This irritated him but he kept quiet.

Sam's phone began to ring and he picked it. When he was through, Daniel asked him, "Can I use your phone briefly?"

"Yes but I don't have much airtime on it."

He gave the phone to Daniel. Daniel called someone and going by how he spoke, Sam guessed the person was his father.

Daniel returned the phone. "Thanks. And thanks again for coming to pick me."

"You're welcome."

Then Sam heard him ask Ann, "Is Sam your cousin?"

"No. He works for my uncle." Ann answered.

"Oh, he works for your uncle? As what?"

"Er … he drives him."

"Oh, he's a driver."

Sam didn't hear Ann's reply. He pursed his lips. He didn't like how they were discussing him as if he was not there and he was becoming increasingly irritated by Daniel.

Daniel continued talking with Ann, "My dad came to Lagos because of me. He will be returning to Warri next week Thursday. I'd like to go with him."

"Is that next week?" Ann asked.

"Yes."

"When will you return to Lagos?"

"I'll stay a couple of weeks and come back."

"Okay."

Soon, they got to Casper Estate. Sam asked Daniel for direction and soon, he stopped the car in front of a beautiful sprawling house. He pressed the horn and an elderly man in a brown uniform appeared.

"Yes? Who are you?"

Daniel opened the door and got down. "Papa D. It's me, Daniel."

"What did you say?"

"It's me, Daniel!"

"Ah, Daniel! You are back!"

"Yes. Papa D!"

The man hurriedly opened the gate and Sam drove in. He brought the suitcases out of the boot. Two teenage boys appeared, followed by a fair-skinned woman who was of an average height and round. They hugged Daniel. Sam heard as Daniel introduced Ann to his mother. Ann knelt down to greet the woman, but the older woman pulled her up and hugged her. Daniel's mother greeted Sam. Papa D pulled one suitcase while one of the teenagers pulled the other.

Ann followed them inside while Sam remained in the car, with his door open and the windows down.

Papa D soon returned. One of the teenagers came out to Sam with a bottle of juice.

"Mummy asked me to give you this."

Sam took it. "Thanks. Tell Mummy I appreciate it."

The boy went back inside.

Thirty minutes after, Ann was still inside the house. Sam was becoming impatient. He turned on the ignition to check the time on the dashboard. The time was 9.05pm. He called Mr. Noah to let him know they were still at Daniel's house.

Eventually, Ann came out with Daniel.

Close to the car, Daniel pulled her hand and stopped her. He held her and began to kiss her.

She giggled, "Oh, please. I have to leave. Sam has to get back to his house."

"He will wait. He's doing his job."

Sam turned and looked at Daniel who didn't see Sam as his back was turned to him. Daniel's mouth was close to Ann's ear.

Ann replied, "No. It's 9.15pm. This is way past his closing time. We'll see tomorrow probably."

He released her and said, "There's nothing like 'probably'. I have to see you tomorrow. I'll be travelling to Warri next week."

"Oh, that's true. I've forgotten. Okay, we'll see tomorrow. What time will you come?"

Walking with her to the car, he answered, "I'll get there by noon."

"Okay. I'll expect you." She told him. She opened the door and sat beside Sam, hooking the seatbelt.

"I'll see you tomorrow." Daniel told her again, closing the door for her.

"Okay."

And to Sam he said, "Goodnight and thanks."

Sam raised his hand in acknowledgment and started the car.

As he pulled out of the compound to the road, Ann spoke,

"Oh, I'm sorry."

"That's fine." He said.

"His parents didn't want me to leave immediately." She explained.

"Hmm. I understand." Sam said.

Ann was trying to make conversations but he remained quiet.

Then she looked sideways at him, "Is everything alright?"

"Yes."

She wasn't convinced. "I'm sorry we took so much of your time."

"That's fine." Then he added, "I'm wondering why Daniel didn't arrange for someone in his family to pick him up from the airport."

"Oh, er ... his mother doesn't drive and his father is sick."

"Hmm. For how long have you known him?"

"We met last month."

"Just last month?"

She nodded. "Yes. Why did you ask?"

"He's a funny guy."

"Why did you say so?"

"I was staying in the car waiting for you and all he could say was - he's doing his job."

Oops! So he heard! "I'm sorry about that. He shouldn't have said that. He didn't mean any harm though. That's how he is."

"I'm sure." He said.

"I apologize on his behalf. Don't be offended."

"I'm not."

Ann relaxed on her seat. "So, where's the Bible you said was in the car?"

He stretched his hand and opened the glove compartment, bringing a Bible out. As she collected it from him, their hands touched, and somehow, he felt an awareness of her.

"My uncle will be wondering why we are taking so long." She commented.

"I've called him."

"Oh, good. What are those Scriptures you said you were going to show me?"

"Er … open to the book of Job, chapter twenty two, verse twenty eight."

"The book of Job -" she said, half to herself as she began to leaf through the Bible. She found that many verses were marked, some in red, some in blue and others in yellow.

"Why did you mark your Bible?"

"The verses matter to me. I mark them so I can easily get them."

"I see. Isn't Job the book after Psalms?"

"It's before Psalms."

Soon, she got it. "I'm there. It reads, 'Thou shall decree a thing, and it shall be established unto thee, and the light shall shine upon thy ways.'"

Sam explained the verse and told her how she would pray.

"I need to write it down." She said and opened her purse, bringing out a pen and a paper.

She wrote the passage down. "What Bible version is this?"

"It's King James version. There are more Scriptures but I'm not very sure of the verses. I will need to open them myself."

"Okay."

She continued to read the chapter. Then she said, "Wow! Look at the preceding verses, from verse twenty one. That's interesting."

Soon, they reached Mr. Noah's house and Sam parked the car.

"Let me have the Bible. I'll quickly show you some Scriptures before we get down." He said and switched the inner light on.

Ann gave the Bible to him.

Opening it, he said, "Here is another one."

He held the Bible on one side and turned so Ann could also read it. Ann moved closer to him and held it on the other side. She looked at the verse as Sam read it.

"And I will give unto thee the keys of the kingdom of heaven, and whatsoever thou shalt bind on earth shall be bound in heaven, and whatsoever thou shalt loose on earth shall be loosed in heaven."

She took her pen and the paper she wrote the first verse on. "That's the book of Matthew, isn't it?"

"Yes, chapter sixteen, verse nineteen." Sam supplied.

She wrote it down.

Sam gave her four more Scriptures and she wrote them down.

Then she said, "It's funny that I've never seen these Scriptures before, even though I read the Bible sometimes and studied Religious Knowledge in High School."

They laughed.

"I'll read them tonight before I sleep." She promised.

He briefly prayed for her, that she would have a good night's rest.

After saying amen, she told him, "Thanks for everything."

They got down from the car and entered the house.

Mr. and Mrs. Noah were still in the living room, and they greeted them. Sam submitted the key of the car and left.

"Your food is on the table." Mrs. Noah told Ann.

"Thank you, Aunty."

She went to the table and as she was eating the chicken and chips, it occurred to her that Sam hadn't eaten, all because of her and Daniel. She shrugged.

Later in her room, she thought of the activities of the day, and Daniel.

She had met some men in SA before meeting Daniel, but she hadn't liked any of them enough to go into a steady relationship.

Then she met Daniel who was five years older than her through a friend. She really liked him and was happy they had come to Nigeria together. He was also a graduate who had travelled abroad to seek a better life, and was there for six years. His father had been asking him to return to Nigeria to join the family's manufacturing business being the first son but he had been reluctant. When his father suffered a minor heart attack four months ago, he had decided to return.

He had told Ann of his plan when they met last month, and she had also told him of her plans to return to the country as well, to Daniel's delight.

The only thing they were yet to settle was the issue of sex. He had told her on their second date that it was important to him and he wanted it.

To Ann, it shouldn't be a big deal as everyone seemed to be doing it, but to be on the safe side, she had discussed with her two friends. The friend in Pretoria had told her to go ahead and do it, claiming that Daniel was a good catch, and sex would keep him interested in Ann and cement their relationship.

"Hey, Annie baby, you have landed on your feet with this man!" She had said. "Just make sure you protect yourself by insisting on condom."

Ann thought so too as Daniel's parents were very rich. Daniel also had a business which his father had set up and was operating for him.

The friend in Johannesburg had told her to wait for some time, to know what Daniel's intentions were. If he wanted marriage, then Ann could do it. She had added that this was to protect Ann's interest so she would not be used and dumped.

Ann had chosen to go by the second friend's advice. She was still a virgin and would want to get to know Daniel better before going into sex. She would not want to have sex with a man who would not marry her or was probably HIV positive, she had thought.

She would want to marry by the age of twenty five or twenty six. As soon as she was sure Daniel wanted marriage with her, she would say yes to sex. Indeed, he was a good catch as her friends had said, being good looking and rich. She had immediately known about his wealth by his lifestyle in SA. And going to his house this evening and meeting his parents, was another confirmation.

She knew Daniel would bring the issue of sex up again tomorrow when he came and she smiled. *That's good. Let him keep asking. It's a sign he likes me. Maybe we'll begin to talk about marriage soon.*

Then her mind went to Sam. Somehow, she liked him. He was easy to talk to. She almost couldn't believe she had allowed him to talk to her about God, prayed and studied the Bible with him.

She thought of reading the Scriptures he gave her but changed her mind. She would read them some other time as she was tired now. With the Bible under her pillow, she got in bed and slept.

She didn't wake up until about 7.30am.

At almost noon, Daniel came to the house in a black latest model Toyota 4-runner SUV.

Sitting in the living room, he looked round at the interior décor and said, "I like your uncle's house. It's beautiful."

"Thank you." She said and sat across from him.

"Would you care for a drink?"

"I want very cold water."

"Alright. Give me a minute." She said and went to the kitchen, opening the refrigerator.

She soon returned with a bottle of water and a glass cup with a long stem on a tray.

He drank it and said, "Let's go out."

"Okay." She easily agreed. "Where do you have in mind?"

"I'd like to visit one of my friends in his office at Ikoyi."

"That's fine. I'll quickly get ready." She said and went to her room.

Soon, she reappeared, taking the glass cup to the kitchen.

"I'm set."

He got up. Halfway to the door, he pulled her hand to stop her.

She looked at him and smiled.

"Spend the night with me."

Still smiling, she asked, "Why?"

"I want us to spend as much time as possible together. I'm travelling next week."

She shook her head. "I can't spend the night with you."

It was his turn to ask why.

"I can't." She said and turned to go.

He pulled her hand back again.

She turned again to look at him. "Daniel, I can't, I mean, not yet."

He released her hand. "Okay. We'll discuss it later."

They went out and walked to the shop to say goodbye to Mrs. Noah.

As soon as Daniel drove out of the compound, he resumed the discussion. "So, what did you mean by you can't?'"

"Daniel," She began.

"What's your excuse this time? When we were in SA, the excuse was that you were not ready for intimacy and that I should give you time. Then it changed to 'We are going to Nigeria together, we should not be in a hurry.' Now we are in Nigeria, what's the excuse this time?"

She laughed. "We have just arrived in Nigeria, Daniel! Why are you so single-minded?"

He didn't laugh with her as he said, "I'm not being single-minded. We are in a relationship … and I'm a man. Do you realize that?"

"Of course, I know. And I'm a woman. Some things are important to me."

"What things?"

"Things such as marriage." There, she had finally told him what she wanted. She waited to hear what he would say.

He laughed. "Marriage? We met only last month, Ann! If we'll begin to talk about marriage, we need to first get to know ourselves well."

He wasn't saying what she wanted to hear, he wasn't saying he would marry her.

"Precisely my sentiments." She told him. "We need to first get to know ourselves better."

"Marriage is a serious issue which should be considered carefully. Sex will make us know if we are compatible and good together."

Ann knew his game. He just wanted sex. She was determined not to give in until he had promised to marry her. But she wouldn't want to push him too much so as not to lose him. She would simply continue to give him excuses, although ... holding back and saying no to sex was becoming increasingly difficult for her considering the pressure he was putting on her.

She shook her head. "I don't really know you yet. I can't have sex."

"Okay, what don't you know about me? I told you about my family and the family businesses. I told you I would want to return to the country and I did. You met my family yesterday. What else?"

She sighed. "Just a little more time, Daniel."

But he wouldn't hear of it. "Everybody does it, Ann. It's normal. You should prove your love to me baby."

"I know but -"

"I care about you."

"And I care about you as well."

"So what's your problem?"

She smiled. "What if I get pregnant?"

"You can't get pregnant."

"Daniel, that's not true. Don't say that. You know it could happen."

"Ann, you know it's just an excuse. We could use protections."

She smiled again. Drawing in a deep breath, she said, "Please, give me a little more time."

"I've given you some time. How much more time are we talking about now?"

"For how long will you be away?"

He shrugged. "I don't know. Maybe a couple of weeks or so."

She shrugged. "Alright."

"Are you sure you don't have something you're trying to hide?"

She laughed. "Like what?"

"I wouldn't know. That's why I'm asking. I mean … for how long am I going to wait for something I'm used to?"

"Now, you're talking. How many ladies have there been before me?"

"I'm a man."

"Answer my question." She insisted.

"That's not relevant."

"Hold on, Daniel. I have a question for you. Do you have anything against marrying a virgin?"

"Nobody cares about that these days." He said with the wave of his right hand.

"Some people still do."

"It doesn't matter to me."

She sighed. "Well, you will soon be back in Lagos."

"Does that mean the case is closed?"

"Daniel, let's wait till you return. It's a promise."

He sighed.

"Look Daniel, the truth is that marriage is important to me. I'm not interested in a casual relationship. I want commitment."

"Well, everything depends on you." He said and pulled a handset from his shirt pocket and showed her. "This is my cell phone. I bought it this morning."

She took it and looked at it, a little surprised that he had bought a cell phone for only himself. If it had been her, she would have bought for him as well. There was a time she went grocery shopping with him in SA and he had bought a lot of things for himself but nothing for her, to her surprise. How could a lady go shopping with him and he would not buy her a thing? He had given her an expensive camcorder some days after though.

She hadn't complained the day of the grocery shopping just as she would not complain now. She would be patient with him. Who knows, he may give me something before he leaves for Warri, she thought.

"It's nice." She said, hiding her feelings. Two could play this game, and she would make sure they played by her rules. "So, what's the number?"

He told her.

"I'd better write it down." She brought her address book out and wrote his number in it.

"Try and get a phone as well so we can communicate easily while I'm away." He told her.

She couldn't hide her feelings any longer. "Where do you expect me to get a phone from?"

He glanced at her.

She went on, "How could you have bought a cell phone for only yourself? I thought you said you cared about me?"

He smiled. "To be honest, it didn't occur to me."

She didn't talk.

"Alright. I'll try and get you one but that may be when I return from Warri."

She calmed down. "Okay. I'll get one as soon as possible."

There was silence for some seconds before he asked, "So, what will you be doing while I'm away?"

"I'm starting work in about ten days' time. I'll go to my parents' house on Sunday, stay a week and come back."

"Why are you going on Sunday, and not tomorrow?"

"That's when my uncle can take me there. He has a wedding ceremony to attend tomorrow."

His phone began to ring and he picked it.

Some fifteen minutes after, they reached his friend's office, stayed about forty minutes and left for another friend's house. He eventually brought her back to Mr. Noah's house at about 7pm.

Mr. Noah had returned from work and was in the living room with his wife. Sam was not in sight and Ann guessed he must have left. Ann introduced Daniel to Mr. Noah as her boyfriend and he left.

Later, Ann asked Mr. Noah, "Uncle, how can I get a cell phone? I will need one."

"I think I have one I can give you."

"Oh, thanks." She said happily.

Mr. Noah turned to his wife. "Open the first drawer of the cabinet in our room. You'll see a pink-colored handset there. Bring it please."

Mrs. Noah stood up, went into the master bedroom and brought a pink-colored Nokia handset in a box. She wanted to give it to her husband but he pointed at Ann.

"Give it to her."

"Thank you very much, Uncle. I'm grateful." Ann said.

"You're welcome. The number is on the yellow card in the box. Bring it out and note it."

"Okay. Thank you." Then she added, "I hope you've not forgotten we're going to my parents' house on Sunday?" Ann asked.

"No."

"By what time would you want me to be ready?"

"We can leave by noon."

"Okay."

 **Chapter 3**

On Saturday, Ann stayed at home. After watching TV for some time, she retired to her room and got in bed. She called Daniel and they talked for some time.

Minutes after the call, she suddenly remembered Sam gave her some Scriptures. Taking her Bible out from under her pillow, she began to check them. She took her pen and underlined them in the Bible. Then she prayed the way Sam told her to. Afterward, she packed a bag which she would take to her parents' house.

After breakfast on Sunday, while waiting for her uncle, Ann was in bed, going through her Bible. She underlined more Scriptures.

At about 11am, Mr. Noah called her and she went to the living room to meet him. He told her he would not be able to take her to her parents' house.

"My wife and I have to be somewhere by 12.30pm." He explained. "I'm sorry. Er … let me find out if Sam is free to take you there."

She sat down while Mr. Noah picked his cell phone and began to press some buttons.

****

Sam was just about leaving the hall where Agape Campus Church held services when his cell phone began to ring. He checked it. It was Mr. Noah.

Inhaling deeply, he picked it. "Hello sir."

"Sam, how are you?"

"I'm fine. Good afternoon sir."

"Good afternoon. Have you finished in church?"

He didn't want to lie so he said, "Yes. We've just finished."

"Oh, good. I was supposed to take Ann to her parents' house but something else has cropped up. Could you do me the favor of taking her there? I'm sorry for the short notice."

Taking a deep breath, he used his right hand to scratch his head lightly. Oh God! He had planned to visit his parents when he learnt the lecture he was to have had been cancelled. And now this! Ann's parents lived at Ota. It would take about one and a half hours drive without traffic to get there.

"Okay sir. What time do you want me to come?" Sam asked.

"If you can come now, that will be fine."

"I was to go somewhere but I will cancel it and come right away."

"Thank you." Mr. Noah said. "I'll be expecting you."

"Okay sir." He answered and pressed the end button.

Sam quickly told his friends that he was leaving. He walked to the bus stop and boarded a bus, on his way to Mr. Noah's house.

About half an hour later, he was standing in front of the house, pressing the bell.

Olu opened the main gate and Sam entered. He saw the BMW and Mrs. Noah's bus in the garage. Mr. Noah must have gone out in the Toyota Corolla.

"Is your daddy at home?" He asked to confirm.

"No. He's gone out with Mommy."

"Where's Ann?"

"She's inside."

"Did your dad leave the key of the car?"

"Yes."

"Okay, bring it and tell Ann I'm around."

"Okay."

Olu went inside.

Soon, he reappeared with Ann. She was pulling her bag behind her. She wore a green cotton blouse on a black pencil skirt which had thigh high cuts.

"Good afternoon." Sam greeted her.

"Good afternoon." She came to meet him where he was standing beside the car. "How are you?"

"I'm okay. And you?"

"I'm fine. Here's the key."

He collected the key, opened the boot of the car and put her bag there. Closing it, he came over to the passenger side and opened the door for her.

"Thank you."

He went to the driver's side, opened the door and entered.

As he started the car, she told him, "Thank you for coming under such a short notice."

He smiled. "Your uncle said you're going to your parents' house."

"Yes. They live at Ota."

"I know the place. I've taken your uncle there a number of times." He said, driving out of the house.

"Oh, really? That's good."

They could hear Olu locking the gate.

"How has your day been?" She asked.

"It's been good. And yours?"

"Good. Did you go to church?"

He smiled. "Sure. It was great. You should come one of these days. What about you, did you go to church?"

"No."

He didn't say anything.

She went on to explain. "I didn't know which one to attend. My uncle's family didn't go anywhere as well. If they had, I would have followed them."

"There's a church not too far to their house. It's a good one. You can go by yourself." He suggested.

She shook her head. "I wouldn't want to go alone. I've just returned to the country. I'd like to tread with care."

"That's reasonable. In that case, you can attend my church, after all, you know me. If I have to, I'll come and pick you with the church bus."

"It's on your campus, right?"

"Yes."

"Er ... I don't know. I can't promise anything but give me the address."

He told her the address, how to get to the venue of the fellowship and times of meetings. She wrote them down.

Her cell phone began to ring. She took her purse and brought it out. It was Mrs. Noah to find out if Sam had come to pick her.

"Yes. We are on the way already."

When the call ended, she asked Sam for his cell phone number and he dictated it. She saved it on her phone.

"Use your phone to call mine, so your number can appear on my screen. I'll save it later."

She did and his phone began to sing God is good by Don Moen.

"Good."

She returned the phone to her purse.

"Am I to wait to bring you back to Mr. Noah's house?" Sam asked.

"No. I'm spending about five days there before I return to Mr. Noah's house. I'll be going to work from there."

"Will you get someone to bring you when you are ready to come back? I'm asking so that if I have to come and pick you, I can make the necessary arrangements."

She shrugged. "I don't know. I may still need your assistance."

"Okay. You have my phone number. Call me or send a text message when you are ready to leave."

"Okay, thanks."

There was about two minutes' silence.

Then he asked, "Have you been enjoying yourself in Nigeria?"

"Yes. It's been good so far."

"Have you read the Scriptures I gave you?"

"Yes. I read them yesterday and this morning. In fact, I have my Bible right here in my purse."

She brought it out.

He was both surprised and impressed. Smiling, he said, "So, it's no longer being kept under your pillow."

"No." She laughed.

He joined in her laughter.

"And I've been marking some verses, like you."

"Really?"

They laughed again.

"That's good. What about the dreams?"

"I haven't had them since then. It's not every day I have them though. I'm sure I will have one again before the end of the week." She said and smiled.

"Does that mean you want to continue to have them?"

"No."

"Then why did you say you're sure it will come again?"

"Well,"

"I told you about the believer's authority on Thursday, and the power of words. It is wrong to say you're sure it will come again. You should say it will not come. Don't expect it."

"Okay. I understand."

"Say it will not come." He told her.

"It will not come."

"Say it like you mean it. It will not come!"

"It will not come!" She said and laughed.

He smiled. "That's better. You have to be conscious of the fact that you have asked Jesus to come into your life. You're no longer the same."

"Okay."

He taught her how she would be praying.

They drove in silence for about a minute before she asked, "Are your parents alive?"

"Yes."

"Where are they?"

"They are here in Lagos."

"Where do they live?"

He mentioned it.

That's a slum! Maybe he lives in one of the fine houses there, she thought.

"So, you come all the way from there?" She asked.

"No. I don't live with them. I live on campus."

"Oh, I see. Do you have a room to yourself or you share?"

"There are two people in each room."

"Oh, I see." She repeated.

Sam spoke again. "I know your paternal grandparents are late, from what you told me the other time. What about your maternal grandparents?"

"They are in my hometown."

They didn't talk for about a minute. Then she said, "Excuse me. I need to call Daniel."

Daniel? Hmm. God, take control, Sam prayed under his breath, frowning slightly

Ann brought her phone out and dialed Daniel's number.

"Hello?"

After exchanging pleasantries, she told him, "I'm on my way to my parents' house."

"Oh good. Er … can I say hello to your uncle?"

"He's not the one driving me. It's Sam. My uncle couldn't go."

"Oh, okay."

When she finished speaking with Daniel, she returned the phone to her purse and began to check the CDs by her seat. After going through all of them, she returned them and relaxed on her seat.

"You will like this one." Sam said and took one of the CDs, giving it to her.

Looking at it, she didn't think she had heard any of the songs before. Yawning, she gave it back to him. "I don't know the songs."

He slotted it into the player and they continued on the journey without talking.

Soon, Sam was pulling into the driveway of her parents' house. Mrs. Sankey who was small in stature, dark in complexion and wore a multicolored boubou was standing outside, in the compound. She rushed over and hugged her daughter. Afterward, she greeted Sam.

Some of the tenants were outside. They knew Ann and came to greet her as well.

Sam assisted Ann to take her bag to the top floor of the two-story building. When they entered the living room,

Mr. Sankey who was there, rose and hugged his daughter before shaking hands with Sam.

"Thank you for bringing her." Mr. Sankey told Sam. He was tall and fair, in his late fifties.

"I thought Layi would bring you." Mrs. Sankey said to Ann.

"Well, he had agreed to bring me but his plans changed at the last minute."

Sam called Ann. "I need to leave immediately."

"Okay. Just a minute."

Before he could say anything, she had taken her bag and left the room.

"Sam, sit down." Mrs. Sankey said.

"Thank you." He said and sat on one of the brown leather sofas. Glancing around, his eyes went to a large painting of Ann's parents on the wall. Sam looked at Ann's mother and could see a definite resemblance between her and Ann even though the latter was light in complexion.

Ann returned with a can of soft drink which she opened and gave Sam.

"Thank you." He said.

When he finished it, he got up and Ann saw him out to the car.

"Thanks for shuffling your plans to accommodate me. I appreciate it." She said as he entered the car.

"The pleasure is mine."

Back in the living room, she sat with her parents to talk.

"Where's Biodun?"

"He went out. He should be back soon." Her mother answered.

She asked after the tenants in the house and decided to visit them. She left, going to the front apartment on the first floor.

Mrs. Afe was at home with her two children, aged five and two. The woman who was a lecturer in a university looked beautiful in the skirt and blouse she wore. She had always dressed well and looked good. She and her husband had moved into the house two years before Ann travelled out.

She hugged Ann.

While talking, Ann noticed an open Bible beside the woman. Remembering that Mrs. Afe and her husband behaved like church people before she travelled, she asked, "Are you a Christian?"

Smiling, the woman answered, "Yes. What about you?"

Ann smiled. "Well ... yes. Someone talked to me on Thursday, a day after I returned to the country, and he asked me to pray which I did."

Mrs. Afe was happy to hear that and she wanted to know how it happened. Ann told her.

She told Ann about her own experience fourteen years ago at the age of twenty. She went on to encourage Ann to continue as a Christian and should not hesitate to ask her questions or discuss with her when necessary.

Ann finally got up to leave at 7.20pm. She returned to her apartment, deciding to visit the other tenants the following day. Shortly after, Biodun came in. The lanky man was a year and a half Ann's junior. Ann gave her parents and brother the gifts she brought from SA.

After breakfast the next day, she visited the other tenants, and afterward, returned upstairs to sit with her parents and talk.

On Tuesday night, Ann had a dream. In it, she was standing in front of a large crowd, talking to them. She wasn't so certain but it seemed she was talking about God and there was so much excitement all around.

When she woke up, she wondered what it was all about. She had never had such a dream before. She tried to forget it but it kept coming back to her mind. She thought of whom to tell about it. If she told her mother, she would only shrug and tell her not to worry, but she was worried! She couldn't tell her father, of course. He didn't seem to have patience to listen to such things.

In the afternoon, she decided to phone Sam and tell him.

He picked it on the second ring. "Hello."

"Hello Sam, it's me, Ann."

"Yes, I know. I believe you are doing well."

"Yes. And you?"

"I'm okay."

"Good."

She heard him telling someone to wait.

"Am I calling at a wrong time? Should I call back?" She asked.

"No, no. You can go on. What's up?"

"I had a dream last night and just thought I should tell you about it."

"Go ahead." He encouraged.

She did.

She heard him make a sound that seemed like a chuckle. "What do you think?" She asked.

"Well, maybe God is trying to reveal His plans for your future."

"What plans would that be?"

"If you were talking to people about God, it means God wants you to talk to people about Him. Simple."

"If that is the case, what am I supposed to do to make it happen?"

"No, you're not the one who will make it happen. All you need to do is to be a good Christian. Be willing to obey God and He will take care of the rest."

He continued talking to her, telling her how to grow spiritually.

In the evening, Mrs. Afe came to see Ann.

"Where are you worshipping on Sunday?" She asked Ann.

"Er, I'm actually going to my uncle's house on Friday. I'm starting work next week." Ann explained.

Just then, her phone rang. It was Daniel.

"Excuse me please." She told Mrs. Afe and left for the balcony to take the call.

She told Daniel about the dream.

"It's nothing." He said without thinking.

He went on to tell her about the many meaningless dreams he'd had.

"So, forget it." He added.

"I'm thinking it's because of the Bible I've been reading these last few days." She confessed.

"Have you been reading Bible?" He asked sharply.

"Yes, and I've been praying. Sam has been talking to me about God."

"Well, I think you should be careful about all that. Don't let Sam put any nonsense in your head!" He warned.

He reminded her he would be leaving for Warri the next day.

When Ann eventually returned to the living room, she told Mrs. Afe. "I'm sorry. I was telling my friend about a dream I had."

"What kind of dream?"

Ann told her.

"Well, you may not fret about the meaning of the dream. Simply go by the word of God. God wants His children to tell others about Him. So, whether or not there's a dream, tell others about God. And if there's more to the dream, God will reveal it with time. So, simply continue to know Him better, be a good Christian." She said, and added, "And ... stay away from sin."

At night, Ann picked her Bible and began to read. She couldn't explain it but she just found she wanted to know more.

The next day, she called Daniel and he told her he was preparing to leave for Warri with his father.

After the call, she phoned Sam and told him she would want to leave on Friday.

"Call and tell your uncle. He needs to know." Sam said.

"I know. I will call him."

She did and Mr. Noah agreed to send Sam to pick her the next day.

On Friday, on their way to Mr. Noah's house, Sam reminded Ann about church on Sunday. "Please, say you'll come."

She thought about it. There wasn't much for her to do on that day anyway.

"Okay. I'll come." She promised.

"Would you like me to come and pick you?"

She liked the idea. "I wouldn't mind."

"Okay. I'll bring the fellowship bus. The service starts at 10am. I'll pick you up by 9am. Do you think you'll be ready?"

"Nine?" She considered it and nodded. "I'll be ready."

"Good."

"Er, how should I dress?"

He smiled. "You're going to church, so dress well."

She opened her mouth to ask what his interpretation of 'dress well' was but changed her mind. There was no need.

"Okay." She said.

"Be ready by nine on Sunday."

"Okay." She repeated.

****

Back on campus, Sam called Ade, the president of Agape Campus Church and told him that a lady who had just arrived from abroad would be worshipping with them on Sunday. He had witnessed to her and she had become a Christian. He would need the bus to pick her up.

"Okay but you won't be able to use the bus to take her back. I will be going out with the sisters' coordinator right after the service to see the pastor we're inviting for our October program." Ade told him.

"That's fine." Sam agreed.

He also informed some of the executive members who were close to him.

"Who is she?" One of them asked.

"She's my boss's niece." He explained.

Going to a nearby store, he bought a bottle of cologne. He hadn't bought new clothes in recent times, so he brought out the shirt that was his best and his best trouser.

He washed, dried and ironed them. He also polished his shoes.

He was to preach on Sunday. He began to prepare and pray, hoping everything would be alright and that Ann would be impressed.

On Saturday morning, he felt it necessary to call and remind her of the Sunday service. Taking his cell phone, he scrolled through his contacts until he got her name. He dialed.

She picked it almost immediately and told him she had not forgotten.

Good.

He decided he would give her a mini book on faith by Kenneth E. Hagin, which he had just bought at Penny Books, a large bookshop by the gate of the University.

That Sunday morning, he woke up early. When it was time, he wore his clothes, used the cologne, took his Bible and the mini book, and left for the president's room to get the bus.

Soon, he was on his way to Mr. Noah's house. He called Ann to let her know he would soon get to the house.

****

Ann ate a light breakfast. Returning to her room, she threw her closet open, searching for an appropriate dress. She realised many of her clothes were not appropriate for church. Some were too short, some showed too much of her thigh while some revealed too much cleavage.

Mrs. Afe came to her mind. She was very beautiful and fashionable but she doubted the woman would wear clothes like these. She should try to be like her.

Ann continued to check her clothes and eventually settled for a light blue dress which she wore immediately. She took her two rings from the bedside table and wore them. Applying her makeup with care, she picked her accessories, shoes and Bible, and went to the living room to wait for Sam.

Mr. and Mrs. Noah were there. Mrs. Noah was having her breakfast while her husband was reading a newspaper. They looked up when she entered.

Mrs. Noah gave her a look of approval. "This looks good on you."

"Thank you, Aunty."

"How will you get to the place?" Mr. Noah asked, peering through his glasses.

"Sam is coming to pick me with the fellowship bus."

He looked back to the newspaper.

Ann sat down and said, "Uncle, I'm starting work tomorrow. Can I go with you in the morning?"

He looked up at Ann again. "That may not be possible tomorrow. I'm leaving late. Tell Sam that I said he should take you there tomorrow."

"Okay. Thank you."

Shortly after, they heard the doorbell ring.

"That must be Sam." Ann said and got up.

"Olu?" Mr. Noah called out.

"No, don't call him. I will open the gate for Sam." Ann said and went out.

At the gate, she asked, "Who is there?"

"It's me, Sam."

She opened the gate wide. Sam entered the bus and drove in. She closed the gate and went to him.

He got down from the bus, happy to see she was fully dressed.

"You're right on time." She said, glancing at her watch. It was 9.05am. "Right on time." She repeated, smiling.

 **Chapter 4**

"Good morning." Sam greeted Ann, taking in every detail of her appearance, from her hair that was packed at the back to her three-inch heel blue shoes. She looked gorgeous. Her light blue gown which was narrow at the waist had a V neckline and a flared skirt. Her accessories matched the color of her gown.

"Good morning." She answered.

Opening the passenger door, she put her purse and Bible on the seat. "I'll just let my uncle know we are leaving."

"I need to greet them." He said and followed her inside.

Sam greeted Mr. and Mrs. Noah.

"Have a wonderful service." The couple told him and Ann.

"Thank you. Goodbye."

Outside, Sam opened the door for Ann and waited for her to enter, before closing the door. He went round to the driver's side and entered.

Driving out of the compound, he said, "I must say I'm a little surprised you're ready."

She smiled. "I like to keep to time."

"That's one thing we have in common there." He said, smiling.

He glanced briefly at her. She looked very beautiful.

She noticed he looked at her and asked, "How do I look?"

"You look great." He said. He just had to tell her.

Smiling broadly, she answered, "Thank you. You're looking great yourself."

He smiled and said thank you.

They drove on in silence for some minutes before he said, "The bus won't be available after the service to bring you back. I'll have to get a cab for you." He explained.

"That's alright. Er ... my uncle asked me to tell you that you'll be taking me to my office tomorrow morning."

"Alright. What time will you like to leave?"

"Er ... by 7am?"

"I'll be there." He answered promptly.

They reached the venue and got down. There were about nine cars parked. The time was 9.50am and service had not started. While Sam was locking the doors of the bus, Ann entered the hall and was surprised to see a crowd of about five hundred. Musical instruments were on the left side of a stage at the front of the hall. Six standing microphones were close to where the musical instruments were while a glass pulpit stood at the center of the stage.

Ann felt a little uneasy and out of place. When was the last time she went to church?

A female usher approached her. As she was leading Ann to a back seat, Sam came over, greeted the lady and told her he would take care of Ann. He led her to the second row in front and showed her a seat.

He put the things in his hands on one of the front seats and went to the choir leader.

"Who is leading the praise and worship?" He asked.

"It's Sylvester." The lady said.

Sylvester was one of the executive members in charge of publicity, and he was allowed to lead praise and worship sometimes.

"Why?" Sam asked with a frown. Why would Sylvester lead songs today, of all days? He wasn't very good, in Sam's opinion.

"Bola was supposed to take it but she has called to say she would be coming late." The choir leader explained.

"But Ore is around. Why not him?" Sam asked.

"Well, er -"

"Have you informed Sylvester?"

"Yes."

Sam took a deep breath. He hoped Sylvester would do it well. "Okay. Which songs will the choir be singing?"

The lady told him.

They were okay and he nodded his approval. "Can Grace do choreography?"

"Under such short notice?" She shook her head.

"She can repeat the one she did last week." He suggested.

Ade came over to join them. When he knew what was being arranged, he laughed.

"President, what do you think?" The choir leader asked Ade.

"Well, call Grace and ask her, so she can get the CD and prepare. She may need to go back to the hostel to get the clothes for it." Ade said.

Sam discussed with Grace and to his relief, she agreed to do it.

He quickly prayed that every aspect of the service would bless everyone present, especially Ann. He sighed, he had done what he could.

The service started promptly at 10am with prayer, followed by praise and worship. Afterward, they sang a hymn.

When first-timers were being recognized, eleven people including Ann, stood up. Some of the members, including Sam went to greet them.

When it was time for the sermon, Ann was surprised to see Sam get up.

His message was titled 'Keep your joy' and he began by reading a Scripture. By the time he finished reading it, the nervousness he'd been feeling since he entered the hall had gone.

Putting his Bible down, he looked at the congregation and pointed, "Keep your joy! This is a message to someone!"

"Talk to me!" A male voice rang out from behind Ann and she looked back, surprised.

"Everybody say 'Keep your joy!'" Sam ordered loudly.

"Keep your joy!" The crowd responded.

The lady beside Ann waved her bulletin and moved her head as she said it. Ann smiled.

As Sam preached on, Ann listened intently, her eyes moving with his every movement. She was seeing another side of him, and she liked it. She was impressed.

At the end of his message, he made a call for those who might want to surrender their lives to God. Three people went to the altar. Ann decided to join them and Sam prayed for them. He also prayed for those who needed healing.

When the service ended, he came to Ann and introduced her to Ade and the sisters' coordinator who they called Mummie.

"We are happy to have you worship with us." Ade told her.

"We hope you'll come again." Mummie said.

Ann smiled and shrugged. Although she enjoyed the service, she didn't want to commit herself in any way.

"Excuse me please. I want to take her to the cafeteria." Sam told them

Passing by the administration buildings and classrooms, Sam took her to the cafeteria. Heads turned as they entered the hall. Sam made her sit at a table near a window at the rear of the hall, and left to buy food for both of them. Some of the students eating greeted Sam. He soon returned with two plates of rice and two bottles of water on a tray. Soft music was playing in the room. Some of the students eating in the hall turned and greeted Sam.

Sitting down, he told Ann to bless the food. She put the fork she had taken down and closed her eyes.

He closed his eyes and listened but didn't hear anything.

"Pray." He said.

"I'm praying."

He opened his eyes and looked at her.

Some people waved at him and he waved back.

"I didn't hear you." He told Ann.

"I pray in my mind."

He smiled. "No. You should pray out. You should say your prayers whether you're praying alone or you're praying with someone. I'll pray for both of us."

As he prayed, Ann listened carefully. The way he prayed was different from what she had ever heard.

She said amen and they began to eat. He asked if she liked the service and she told him she liked every part of it.

"I like the way you preached. The message was good. It was for me."

Sam smiled. *Thank You Lord.* He had been very nervous before he came up to preach but the moment he collected the microphone, the nervousness disappeared.

She went on. "I like the praise and worship as well. I learnt some songs. In fact, I wrote them down."

That was another prayer answered, Sam thought.

She took her Bible, opened it and brought a paper out.

As she held the paper up, Sam noticed the rings on her fingers.

"Did someone give you those rings you're wearing?"

She shook her head. "No. I bought them."

"I see."

She began to sing the songs.

"Wow! You are a fast learner." He commented.

She smiled.

"And you have a great voice. I didn't know you could sing."

She laughed and informed him, "I actually like to sing. I was in the choir in High School."

"Wow!"

There was silence for some seconds before he asked, "You came out during the service when the altar call was made. That was good. Why?"

She shrugged. "I just felt I needed to do it ... felt I needed to get close to God."

"I'm happy to hear that. You did the right thing. But last week Thursday, on our way to the airport to pick

Daniel, you prayed and surrendered your life to God, remember?"

She nodded.

He went on. "If a person has sincerely given his or her life, the person doesn't need to keep coming out to do it again. If after the conversion, the person still feels he or she is not close enough or needs to do more for God, the person should simply pray concerning that need. Or if there's sin in that person's life, the person should pray and repent, and ask God for forgiveness. Do you understand?"

She nodded. "Yes."

"So, maybe I should ask, did you mean your prayers, have you given your life to God?"

Without hesitation, she nodded again and said, "Yes, I meant every prayer I prayed today. Even though I prayed on Thursday but I didn't fully grasp the meaning. I didn't fully understand what I was doing or how I was supposed to live as a Christian, but now I know. I can say that I've given my life to God."

Sam was very happy. Smiling broadly, he said, "Good. Now you have become a child of God. You don't need to keep coming out to do it again. Simply obey God and love Him."

She nodded severally, to show she understood.

"I hope you'll come again to our fellowship."

She smiled. "Most likely."

He gave her the mini book on faith. "You will learn a lot from this book."

"Thanks."

Some of the fellowship members entered the cafeteria and saw them. They came over, greeted them and left.

"I heard all of you speaking in a foreign language during the service. What was that about?" She asked.

"That was speaking in tongues." He answered and went on to explain it to her.

Interested, she asked if she could be prayed for the following Sunday to speak in tongues and he said yes.

That meant she would come next Sunday, Sam thought. He was happy she was showing so much interest in the things of God.

Her cell phone began to ring and she checked it. It was Daniel.

"It's Daniel. Excuse me." She told Sam as she pressed okay.

While she was on the phone, Sam was thinking. Her relationship with Daniel would be a hindrance to her spiritual growth. Should he bring it up with her? He thought against it immediately. He shouldn't. She was a new believer and today was her first day in church. Bringing such an issue up might scare her away and make her go back. If she continued to grow, she would soon realize that a relationship with a non-believer was wrong and she would do the right thing. He made a mental note to pray for her in the night.

"I'm in Livingston University. I worshipped in Sam's church." Sam heard her tell Daniel.

She went on. "No, no. It was okay. I like the service - no, they are different - no, it's different from those ones."

Sam wondered what Daniel was telling her. *God, make Ann stand in You*, he muttered under his breath.

About five minutes after, she was off the phone and they continued talking.

Three men who had been eating stood up. On their way out, they called out to Sam.

"Pastor Sam! Who is the beautiful lady with you?"

"You have a query to answer when you get to the room."

"We have seen you!"

Different people teased him as they came in and out. Ann was smiling.

She finished eating and told him, "I enjoyed the food. Thanks."

When she was ready to leave, he walked with her across the campus, passing by a splashing fountain. They were talking. They got to a point where they had to cross the road. A car was coming and they stopped to let it pass. As soon as it did, they crossed and continued talking. They reached the main road where she could get a cab. After some minutes, they got one. Sam negotiated with the driver and paid the fare.

"No, you shouldn't pay for me." Ann protested.

He smiled, "I've already paid."

He couldn't afford to be so generous but he felt paying for her was the right thing to do, at least, today.

"Thanks." Ann said, touched by the gesture.

****

As Ann went home, she thought about everything that had happened. Even though she liked everything about the service, she had felt a little out of place. She, a graduate who had just come from abroad, having to sit and fellowship with students. They were very warm and friendly though. Sam also had obviously gone out of his way to make her comfortable. He seemed to be nice and responsible. He also appeared to be a little popular as many people in the cafeteria greeted him.

She smiled as she remembered some of the comments of the people as they teased him about her.

Well, worshipping with them should be okay as it was a Christian fellowship and it was all about God.

She began to think about the decision she had made to follow God. She hoped it would not turn out to be a mistake. From what she knew, people's lifestyles changed when they became true Christians. Was she ready for that? And what would people say when they got to know that she had changed for real? What would her friends in SA say? What about Daniel? He definitely would not like it. Would she be able to handle the changes, questions and ridicule that would surely come?

Sighing, she took the mini book Sam gave her and began to read.

Some minutes later, she got home. In her room, she called Sam to let him know she got home safely.

****

Sam's cell phone began to ring as he entered his room. He pulled it from his shirt pocket and checked. Seeing it was Ann, he quickly picked it and sat down, smiling. The call lasted about two minutes. He decided to set a special ringtone for her name so he would immediately know it was her.

He liked her and was glad she seemed to be growing as a believer but he was certain her relationship with Daniel would be a hindrance. God would have to do something about it. He began to pray for her eyes of understanding to be enlightened and that God would talk to her concerning Daniel.

****

On Monday morning, Ann woke up early and turned off her alarm which was due to sound in four minutes. She took her bath and thereafter took custard meal. Returning to her room, she wore a brown skirt suit with a matching camisole.

Sam arrived at 6.50am. While waiting for her in the car, he adjusted the rearview mirror to check that he looked okay.

Soon, Ann appeared and they left in Mr. Noah's BMW.

"Thanks again, for everything." Ann said.

"My pleasure."

They drove in silence for some minutes.

Ann looked at him to ask a question but found him muttering under his breath.

Tilting her head to one side, she asked, "What are you doing?"

"Praying."

"Oh, I see."

"You want to say something?" He asked and glanced her way with a smile. He felt a connection developing between them which he couldn't quite explain.

"Not really. Go on." She opened her purse and brought a book out.

Sam took his eyes off the road briefly to look at her and saw the book he had given her in her hands.

"Have you started reading it?"

"Yes. I started yesterday."

He didn't say anything.

She began to tell him about some of the things she had read in the book and how much she liked the book.

It took about thirty minutes to get to First Place Investment Company. Sam drove inside the large compound and stopped by the entrance of the white high rise building for Ann. The building had floor-to-ceiling glass windows.

"Have a nice day." He told her before driving off.

Ann walked in and saw a man who seemed to be in his forties at the reception desk in the lobby. With a smile, she greeted him and told him where she was going.

"Tenth floor." The man said.

"Thank you."

She pressed the call button for the elevator and waited. Soon, it arrived. She entered and pressed number ten button. The elevator doors closed and she was silently taken up. On the tenth floor, the doors opened and she stepped out on marble floor. Glancing around, she saw the name of the company by a large door. She walked down a long corridor, reached the door and opened it, stepping inside.

A woman at the reception smiled and said, "Good morning. How may I help you?"

"I'm here to see the General Manager."

"Do you have an appointment?"

"Yes. Er … actually, I'm a new staff."

"May I have your name please?"

Ann told her.

"Alright. Please sit down." The woman said, indicating the single light brown colored chairs on a side.

Ann thanked her and sat down on one of the chairs while the woman made a call to the General Manager on the intercom to confirm.

Replacing the receiver, the woman stood up and told Ann to follow her.

They walked through the office till they reached a glass door and the woman tapped lightly on the door.

"Come in." A male voice said.

She turned the doorknob, opened it and told Ann to enter.

Ann walked into the room with modern office furnishings.

"Good morning sir." She greeted the man.

"Good morning, Miss Sankey." The man with grey mustache said. "Please sit down."

Shortly after, Ann was introduced to the other nineteen staff members.

The office which Ann would share with a man, James, was in a corner. Ann had on her assigned mahogany table a computer and an intercom. There was a white cabinet beside her chair.

She tried to familiarize herself with James who was in his late thirties, of an average height and balding. While they were talking, she noticed the picture of him and his wife on his table. Her eyes searched the scatter of files and stacks of papers on the table and she saw a small brown leather-bound Bible.

She discovered he was a Christian. When she declared herself a young Christian, the light-complexioned man told her of a lunch-hour fellowship across the road, which he and another staff attended regularly.

"It's just for thirty minutes. We start at 1pm and by 1.30pm on the dot, it's over. I've been attending the fellowship for almost two years. It's always refreshing."

Ann was interested. "I won't be able to go today though."

"That's understandable."

She turned to the computer on her table and began to study her work.

About an hour later, a middle-aged woman with some grey hair entered the office. James introduced her as Lara, the woman who attended the lunch-hour fellowship with him.

The day went by quickly, and soon, it was time for her to go home. James volunteered to drive her to a place where she got a cab that took her home.

The following morning, she went with her uncle, with her sitting beside Sam in front. She didn't talk much with Sam. She noticed he was praying quietly again. She too began to talk to God quietly, committing the day into His hands.

Later in the day, she received a text message from Sam, asking how she was, and she replied that she was okay.

On Wednesday evening, he called her to say hello. She told him of the lunch-hour fellowship and he encouraged her to attend.

On Thursday, Ann went with James and Lara for fellowship. By the entrance, she saw a woman selling books and Bibles. Ann planned to buy a bigger Bible. Immediately after the fellowship, she came there and bought a New Living Translation Bible.

The next day, Sam called her again in the evening to find out if she attended the lunch-hour fellowship.

"Yes, I did. I even bought a Bible there."

Sam liked that.

On Friday evening, he called to ask if she would be coming on Sunday for service.

"I guess so."

"Why did you use the word 'guess'?" He asked.

She chuckled. "Er ... can I be honest with you?"

"Please do." He told her immediately.

"I felt a little awkward the other time, having to sit with students. It shouldn't matter though. I'll come."

He laughed. "I understand but let me tell you, half of those students are your age or older than you. And quite a number of them are married. Also, don't forget that some of them work. You know at least one of them who works."

They laughed.

She nodded and said, "That's true."

"So, you don't need to feel out of place."

"I'll be there." She promised. "Don't bother to come and pick me up. I'll find my way."

"Do you drive?"

"Yes."

"Why don't you ask your uncle to allow you use the BMW?" He suggested.

"I've thought of it but -" she hesitated.

"Well, whatever you decide. Let me know if you need my assistance."

"Okay, I will."

Sunday morning, after a light breakfast, she wore a yellow blouse on a long black velvet skirt. She applied makeup to her face and wore yellow jewelries. Then she took her rings from the table. As she was about to put them on her fingers, she stopped. Did she need to wear them? Sam hadn't said anything against the use of them but she had sensed his disapproval.

Returning them to the table, she wore black shoes, took her new Bible and black purse, and left for Agape Campus Church. It was Ade who preached.

After the service, Sam called Ade and Mummie. Together, they prayed for Ann and she began to speak in tongues. When they were through, the four of them walked across the campus to the cafeteria and ordered meals and soft drinks which Ade paid for.

When Ann used her left hand to carry her cup, Sam noticed she was not wearing the rings. Surprised, he smiled.

They talked as they ate.

Ann noticed the wedding ring on Mummie's finger. "Are you married?"

"Yes."

"Oh, really?" Ann was surprised. "You don't look it."

"I'm twenty six." She said, smiling.

"Wow!" Ann exclaimed. "One wouldn't have been able to guess that you're married though."

"In two or three months, everyone will be able to guess. It will be obvious." Ade said.

They laughed.

Smiling, Ann asked, "Are you pregnant?"

"Yes." Mummie replied.

"Wow! Congratulations. Where's your husband?"

"He's in Dublin."

"When did you get married?"

"Two months ago." Mummie answered. "Are you in a relationship yourself?"

"Yes." Ann answered and smiled.

Sam frowned.

"That's good. Where is he?" Mummie asked.

"We returned from SA together. He went to Warri. He will be back soon."

"Is he a Christian?"

Ann smiled, "Well, he's a Christian, I mean, as in 'a Christian', but he's not a believer like us."

"Hmm."

Mummie, Sam and Ade exchanged a look.

Mummie went on. "Well, the fact that he's not a believer like you means a lot. That means something is not yet in place. Now that you're a true Christian, whoever you are in a relationship with must also be a true Christian."

"Okay." Ann nodded to show she understood.

Mummie added, "And for us Christians, there should not be sex until we are married. A man may say 'Oh, sex is okay if we love each other.' That's not true. The fact that a man and a woman love each other does not make premarital sex right. Why? Because they are Christians. Some may even say that sex is okay because they are going to get married eventually."

Ann was surprised. Mummie was talking about the issues in her relationship with Daniel. So, those ideas she had about sex were wrong and she never knew!

Mummie was still talking. "The fact that they plan to get married does not make sex right. Sex is right only in marriage."

Ann thought she'd better ask them concerning the issue of sex, so she would know what to tell Daniel. He definitely would talk about sex when he returned from Warri.

She spoke. "I have some questions about sex. Some people say that sex will make a relationship better. Is that true?"

"In marriage, yes. Outside marriage, no." Mummie answered. "When there's no marriage, sex brings a lot of confusion and complications. There's no commitment. Why should a lady have sex with a man who has not put a ring on her finger anyway?"

Ann spoke again. "People also say that sex is important before marriage so they can know if they are compatible. Is that so?"

Mummie shook her head. "That's a big lie! You don't need to have sex to know whether or not you're compatible. Sex is not and can never be the true test of real love before and even after marriage."

Ann smiled. "Alright. Here's another question. Someone said that men don't want to marry virgins, that they don't care about it anymore. Is that true?" She looked at Sam.

"That's not true. I care about it. If I could get a virgin to marry, I'd be very happy." Sam said and looked at Ade.

"I care about it as well." Ade said. "Only men who want to take advantage of naive girls say that, and it's simply to get their way. What they capitalize on is the ignorance and innocence of those girls. They use them and dump them."

Mummie spoke. "You may also hear people say that everybody is doing it."

Sam shook his head.

Mummie went on. "It's not true. Not everybody is doing it. I married as a virgin, and I know quite a number of men and women who are still virgins and have purposed to remain that way until they are married."

Ann took a deep breath. "Er ... there's the case of a lady. Er ... a man is giving her pressure for sex, I mean serious pressure. I think the lady wants the man to promise her marriage before she gives in. What do you think?"

They smiled.

Ade spoke. "The lady does not know about men. She is naive."

Sam and Mummie nodded.

Ade went on. "A man can easily promise to marry her, and as soon as he's had his way, dump her. A promise is nothing. The lady should not do it until she's married. Are the people you talked about Christians?"

"Er ... I'm not sure." Ann hedged.

"Well,"

"I think the lady is a Christian." Ann said.

"If the lady is a Christian, she should not have sex until she's married, and she should not be in a relationship with a man who is not a Christian. People can do whatever they like but the moment a person claims to be a child of God, things must be different. There must be a change."

Sam suspected Ann's question was about her and Daniel. He said, "A man may ask a lady to prove her love by having sex with him. The lady should let him know that sex is not a proof of love. Many people such as commercial sex hawkers have sex without love."

Mummie spoke again. "The important thing is to be willing to obey God. There are many lies and excuses people give, but if a person is committed to God, he or she cannot make a mistake."

Ade suddenly laughed and said, "I hope you don't feel scared."

Ann smiled and said, "No."

She had actually learnt some vital lessons. Realizing that the advices of her friends in SA about sex were wrong, she was happy she had not had sex with Daniel. Her heart was a little troubled though. She would have to think about her relationship with Daniel later.

"Good." Ade said. "I'm happy to hear that because I know God has great plans for you. Your future is bright. You need to know the truth and the truth will set you free. Have you seen that verse in the Bible?"

Ann shook her head.

"It's in the book of John, chapter eight verse thirty two."

Taking her Bible, Ann opened it. Then she took her pen and underlined the verse.

Ade laughed. "I like that."

Sam took a deep breath before sending a word of prayer to God on Ann's behalf. *Lord, uphold her.*

They continued talking. When they finished eating, Mummie invited Ann to her room.

On the way to the red brick building, Ade excused himself and left.

"Where is your hostel?" Ann asked Sam.

He pointed. "That is it. You can see my room some other time."

"Okay. I like that book you gave me. Can I get some other titles?"

"Sure." Sam said. "I have two other ones I can give you. I'll bring them tomorrow."

He went with them to Mummie's room. Ann didn't stay long. Mummie accompanied them to the gate.

Sam pointed at a building. "That's Penny Books. I buy books and CDs there."

"Is it open?"

Sam shook his head. "No. It doesn't open on Sunday."

Ann soon got a cab and left.

In the cab, she remembered what Mummie said concerning her relationship. She took a deep breath. What should she do? Was Daniel a true Christian? She didn't think so. Would she have to leave him?

Not having answers to these questions, she inhaled deeply again, suddenly feeling tired. She wouldn't want to think about an issue as serious as that right now. It could wait till later, after all, Daniel was still in far away Warri.

****

In the night, Sam found himself thinking about Ann. He was happy she was growing up in the Christian faith. She was the last person he had expected to become one. He smiled.

She was a likeable person. She was friendly and open, quick to smile and laugh.

****

On Monday morning, as soon as Ann entered the car, Sam gave her the two mini books.

"Oh, thanks." She said.

Every morning, she went with her uncle and Sam, getting down at her office first before they proceeded to theirs. In the evening, she and Sam talked on phone. She also spoke with Daniel.

On Sunday, she was back at Agape Campus Church for service.

****

On Saturday afternoon, Ann was in the living room with Olu and Mrs. Noah when Mrs. Noah received a call.

She suddenly shouted, "Kate did what?"

Ann and Olu looked at her.

What happened to Aunty Kate? Ann wondered. She was close to the lady who was seven years older than her. Kate was Mrs. Noah's niece and she used to live with Mrs. Noah.

As Ann listened, she brushed crumbs of scotch egg from her blouse and jeans skirt.

"She wanted to commit suicide? Why?" Mrs. Noah asked.

Aunty Kate wanted to commit suicide? Ann was surprised.

Mrs. Noah didn't talk for some minutes as she listened to the caller. Then she said, "Why should she attempt to take her life simply because she was jilted four months to her wedding? That was a silly thing to do! If a person commits suicide, that's the end!"

The woman was quiet for some minutes again. Then she spoke, "So, how's she? - she's left the hospital? - okay - she's with you? - okay, I'll come and see her - okay, bye."

When Mrs. Noah got off the phone, Olu asked, "What happened to Aunty Kate?"

Mrs. Noah explained that Kate had attempted to kill herself because the man she was to marry said he was no longer interested in getting married to her.

"Is it Uncle Jude?" Ann asked.

"Yes."

Ann was surprised. They seemed to really love each other. What could have gone wrong?

"Why did he jilt her four months to their wedding?" She asked.

"My sister said he told Kate he has fallen in love with a younger lady in his office." Mrs. Noah explained.

"That's terrible!" Ann said. "Poor Aunty Kate."

Mrs. Noah got up. "I have to go and see her right now."

She took her phone and called her husband to tell him she had to go out to see her sister and Kate.

When she returned later in the evening, Ann asked how Kate was.

"Would you believe she almost killed herself?" She told Ann in disbelief.

"I'd love to see her as well." Ann said.

"I'm going there again tomorrow afternoon."

"Can I come with you?" Ann asked.

"It's okay." Mrs. Noah said.

"I will be back from church by 2pm."

"Okay, I'll wait for you."

The next day after the service, Ann told Sam she would need to leave immediately as she would be going with Mrs. Noah to see her niece who had tried to kill herself.

"That's sad. What happened?"

Ann explained and then said, "Give me some Scriptures I can use to encourage her and which she can meditate on."

Sitting together on a side, Sam wrote some Scriptures for her.

"Thanks. I will call you later to let you know how it goes." She told him.

"I'll expect your call."

Sam told the others he was leaving to see Ann off.

 **Chapter 5**

At home, Ann met Mrs. Noah relaxing in the living room.

"I'm back." She said.

Mrs. Noah got up to prepare herself and soon they left in the BMW, with Mrs. Noah behind the wheel.

Kate's mother took them into the bedroom where Kate was. She was in bed and the TV was on.

They greeted her and asked how she was. After some time, Mrs. Noah and Kate's mother went to the living room.

Ann came closer to Kate and said. "Aunty, everything will be fine."

She looked at Ann with a frown. "That's what everyone is saying but how? How could Jude do this to me?"

Ann nodded to show understanding. "What he did really doesn't make sense. It's sad and unfortunate ... but you must accept it and take things easy. It's not the end of life."

Kate shook her head sadly. "It is for me."

"No, it's not." Ann countered, "or maybe I should say that it shouldn't be. If he doesn't want to marry you, so be it. It's his loss. You are unique, beautiful and wonderfully created. Why would you kill yourself? It's a painful experience, no doubt, but there are other ways of handling the pain."

"I really can't understand it ... after being together for four years!" Kate raised her right palm and spread out four fingers. "And only four months to our wedding?!" She lamented. "I'm thirty-one! Where will I start from?!" Tears gathered in her eyes.

Ann took her hand and said, "It's okay, Aunty. If he left you, it simply means you were not meant for each other. He didn't love you enough. You should be happy it happened now and not after marriage. Some men continue to see their ex-lovers after marriage, and the marriage eventually collapses. I'm sure you don't want that."

It was as though Kate didn't hear her as she said, "I didn't know he was seeing another lady. I never suspected him, never doubted his love. I thought everything was fine ... thought we had a good relationship ... thought he loved me as much as I loved him. He must have taken me for a fool."

"Aunty, it's sad but just let him go." Ann advised. "Move forward. You will find love again."

Kate shook her head.

Ann spoke again and pointed out, "You were not right for each other. The relationship might have looked good, but some things were obviously not in place. Some things were wrong."

Kate sighed and shook her head again. "I think I'm through with the issue of marriage. I won't get married."

Ann smiled a little, "You will get married. Time will heal your heart. You will meet another man."

"No, I won't! What about the shame and the pain? What about the trouble of starting all over again? This is the second time this is happening to me." Kate revealed.

"I don't think I can go through it again." She shook her head.

"You will find another person to love." Ann assured her.

"No! If they could leave me, maybe I'm the problem. It may be that I'm not a good person."

Ann smiled. "Aunty, that is not true. You're a good person."

"Well, maybe I'm not good enough! This is the second time I'm being dumped ... or maybe I should say the third time." Kate said. "I was supposed to marry a man at the age of twenty-four, but he suddenly began to maltreat me, and we had to break up."

"These things can happen to anyone." Ann said.

"But it doesn't happen to everyone. My friends are married. Something must be wrong with me!"

Ann considered Kate's statement and thought she might be right. Clearing her throat, she said, "Whatever the case may be, it's normal to feel bad but please, don't give in to pain or self-pity. That won't solve the problem. It's a painful experience but … life has to go on."

"Hmm. Life has to go on." Kate repeated in a sad way and nodded.

Ann spoke again. "Yes, life has to go on. There are many things a person can do to handle disappointment, but suicide is not one of them ... or maybe I should say that suicide is a wrong way of handling it. I mean, why should you kill yourself? It's not worth it! No man is worth it!" She paused to allow the words sink in.

She continued, "Aunty, if a person commits suicide, that's the end. Once it's done, it's done." She waived her right hand from left to right, to show finality. "You can't undo it ... you can't change your mind ... but I'm sure that deep in your heart, you don't really want to die. What you want is for him to change his mind and come back to you. If you commit suicide however, you can never have him again. Suicide is the end, there's no coming back, and there's nothing like reincarnation.

"What do you mean there's nothing like reincarnation? I believe in it."

Ann smiled. "No Aunty. There's nothing like reincarnation. According to the Bible in Hebrews chapter nine verse twenty-seven, it's appointed for people to die once, and after this the judgment."

There was silence for some seconds. Ann was thinking of what else to say, to convince her that her belief in reincarnation was erroneous, but she couldn't think of a Scripture.

Kate thought of arguing with her concerning reincarnation but decided against it. Reincarnation was the least of her problems right now. Thinking about Jude's insensitive treatment of her got her upset.

She swore and said angrily, "Jude will pay for this! I will make him regret it!"

"No, Aunty, don't make him regret it. You shouldn't do that. Don't try to revenge or become nasty. As I said before, if he left you, it's because he's not meant for you. There's no need to become a bitter woman, or nasty. Let him go." Ann said.

Bringing out her Bible from her handbag, Ann opened it to Romans chapter eight verse twenty-eight, and said, "Here, the Bible says 'And we know that God causes everything to work together for the good of those who love Him and are called according to His purpose for them'. You see, all things work together for good."

"What does that mean?"

"It means that God will take whatever is happening, including satan's plans, and turn them around in favour of His children, to bring about His will and master plan."

"How?"

"God is powerful, and He's working on behalf of His children."

Kate looked away, disinterested. *What good can come out of this?*

Ann brought out a paper on which she had written some Scriptures. Opening her Bible to the verses, she read, and explained them to Kate. Afterward, she prayed for her.

"I will come back later in the week to see you." Ann promised.

"Thank you very much."

At home in the evening, Daniel called Ann.

"So, when are you coming back?" She asked him.

"I should be back this week."

"When?"

"I will be back in Lagos by Wednesday."

"Alright. I'll expect you." Ann said.

"And don't forget that you made a promise to me before I left."

Ann chuckled. She had a surprise for him when he returned. She had changed and sex was definitely out of it. They would need to talk about their relationship and she would have to talk to him about church.

Soon after Daniel's call, Sam phoned her.

"So, how was your visit to Kate's house?"

Ann told him.

In the night, she found herself praying and thinking about her relationship with Daniel. If she let Daniel go, when would she get another man? She would be twenty four years soon.

"Lord, help me." She prayed.

On her way back from the office on Wednesday, Ann stopped to see Kate as she had promised, and encouraged her more. She noticed that Kate looked better than she did on Sunday.

Then Ann told her, "Let's go to church together on Sunday."

Kate shrugged.

"Please say yes." Ann said. "I will come and pick you."

"Okay." Kate agreed. "Going to church will be better than staying at home, worrying and crying. Where is the church?"

"It's Agape Campus Church. It's in Livingston University. You will like it."

Kate shrugged. "It wouldn't hurt to attend."

Ann smiled. "It wouldn't. It would help, trust me."

"Er, I hope I won't look too old among those students?"

"No. There are many mature people among them. Some of them are even married." Ann said.

"Okay. Er, I started my vacation yesterday. I'm thinking of going somewhere to rest. Maybe I'll go to church with you when I return."

"When will that be?" Ann asked.

"My vacation is three weeks. I should be back by September 15. Just call to remind me."

"I will."

The next day, which was August 26, Ann got a pay advice that her salary had been paid into her account at Focus Bank which was just across the road. She left the office and went to the bank to withdraw some money. While she waited to be attended to, one of the bank officials called her.

"Hello." She responded.

The man, who was of an average height and dark, came to her. "It seems I've seen you a number of times at the lunch-hour fellowship."

"It's possible. I do attend." She looked at him closely but didn't recognize him as over one hundred people usually attended the fellowship.

"I come there too." He said and offered his hand. "I'm Emma, Pastor Emma actually. I'm a pastor in my church."

"Ann." She told him as they shook hands.

They talked briefly.

Soon, Ann got the money and returned to office. She had heard about the importance of paying tithe and she removed ten percent of her salary, putting it in an envelope, to be taken to church on Sunday. She knew the money would be handy to them in the fellowship.

On her way home, she received a call from Daniel.

"Are you back in Lagos?"

"No." He answered tiredly.

"I thought you said you would be back this week."

"Yes, so I said but my father had another heart attack yesterday evening."

"Oh!" Ann exclaimed. "Not again!"

"Yes."

She heard a sigh from his end.

"How is he?"

"He's in the hospital. That's where I'm calling from."

"Oh, I'm sorry."

"The poor man." Daniel said. "I can only hope he doesn't die now."

"He won't. I'll be praying for him."

He sighed again. "With the way things are, I can't come to Lagos yet."

"I understand. What about your mother?"

"She's here now. She arrived this afternoon."

"Oh, I'm sorry to hear that. Everything will be alright."

"Can you come over?" He asked.

"Come over? To Warri?"

"Yes."

She laughed. "Daniel, I'm working, remember?"

"I miss seeing your face."

She would love to see him as well but ... she sighed.

Daniel went on. "As soon as he's much better, I'll be back."

"Alright." She said.

"So, what have you been doing?"

She took a deep breath. She would need to let him know she had become a true Christian now, and she sincerely hoped he too would become one. She had to try to talk to him.

"Er, Daniel, I told you Sam has been talking to me about God -"

"And I told you to be careful."

Picking her words carefully, she said, "Yes, you did but I realized I needed to get close to God which is what I'm doing. I now go to church regularly."

He was silent for some seconds before he said, "Well, there's nothing wrong with going to church as long as they don't fill your head with wrong doctrines and stupid stuff!"

She smiled. "They are born again. I am born again. They don't have wrong doctrines or stupid stuff. We do only what the Bible says."

"I'm not sure I like the sound of this though."

She laughed. "Everything is fine, Daniel. I'm fine."

"I hope you haven't changed in any way."

She chuckled. "Haven't you been listening to me? That's the whole point! Things have changed with me."

"In what way?"

"I'm now a child of God, and I've stopped doing some things I used to do."

"How does this affect us, me?"

"Positively."

"How?"

"This is the right way, Daniel. You need to follow it too. You need to -"

He sighed and cut her off. "Let's talk about this later. I have enough to worry about right now."

That's true. She should not push him about church.

On Sunday, Ann got a cab and went to church. When it was time for tithe, she gave hers.

As usual, Ann, Sam, Ade, Mummie and one other man went to the cafeteria. As they walked in, Ann pulled Sam's hand.

He stopped.

"I'll pay for our meals. How much do we need?"

He told her.

She opened her purse and counted the money out.

"Thanks." He said, collecting the money.

"I paid my tithe during service. I just thought I should let you know."

"Okay. God bless you."

About an hour after, they walked out of the hall.

"Are you in a hurry to get back home?" Sam asked Ann.

"Not really."

"Will you like to see my room now?" He asked Ann. "We can all go together." He turned to look at Mummie.

"Alright." Mummie said.

They walked in the direction of his hostel.

Kofi, Sam's roommate was around and Sam introduced him to Ann.

Sitting on a chair in Sam's corner, Ann looked round the small room. There was a faded towel by the foot of Sam's bed, and some bowls and buckets that should have been thrown away. The pale blue bed sheet was also faded. There was a medium size TV on a wooden platform in his corner.

She looked at Sam, "Do you have a photo album?"

"Er … I have some pictures but I've not put them in an album."

"Bring them." Mummie said.

He brought his collections out and gave them to Ann. As Ann looked at them, she passed them to others. Sam identified and told her of the people in the pictures. Most of the pictures were not recent and from what she saw, he came from a very humble background.

"Where did you take this?" Ann asked, holding a photograph.

"This was taken in my parents' living room." He answered.

Ann looked at the picture closely, the leather on the four single chairs in the room was torn. The floor had no rug and the wall was dirty.

She took another picture.

"That's my father." He told her.

The man, who could be in his sixties held a hoe. Ann guessed he must be a farmer but she didn't bother to say anything about it.

"How many siblings do you have?" She asked.

"I have four, all boys. I'm the first born." He explained.

"Wow!" She exclaimed.

"That's a lot of responsibility." Ade said and laughed.

"And a lot of work for your mother especially." Mummie added.

Sam laughed. "You can say that again."

When Ann was leaving, Sam gave her two CDs.

In bed later, Ann thought about Sam's family. They were obviously poor. Yet, Sam had developed himself, and tried to give to others from the little he had. She decided she would start giving him things too, to assist him.

On Wednesday, the first day of September, Ann was in the office when she received a text message from Sam.

God will edify, identify, modify, beautify, sanctify, purify, glorify, gratify, magnify, dignify, satisfy and fortify you in this new month.

Ann laughed. She liked it. She had also received a text message from Lara in her office and decided to forward it to Sam.

New day, new moment, new season, new life, new mercy, new grace, new hope, new strength, new peace, new joy, new song. God will make all things new for u in this new month, Ann.

Almost immediately, she received a reply from him.

Amen. Tanx and have a nice day.

She forwarded the message from Lara to Daniel as well, whom she had called everyday to ask how his father was.

On Saturday, she went to a store to get a gift for Mrs. Noah whose birthday would be on Monday. She saw towels of good quality and her mind went to Sam. He needed to change his towel. She took one and threw it in her cart. She also picked a box of cutleries and a set of glass cups for him. And for Mrs. Noah, she picked a wristwatch of good quality.

After service on Sunday, Ann told Sam she had some things to give him and he told the President he had to leave with Ann immediately. They left and went to the cafeteria again. When she said she didn't want to eat, Sam bought two bottles of soft drinks and sat opposite her on a table for two. She gave him the plastic bag containing the things she bought for him.

"These are for you." She brought them out.

He was surprised. "For me? Wow! I'm speechless! I don't know what to say." He said, checking the things.

She smiled. "All I want to know is if you like them and you will use them."

"Of course, I like them and I will use them. Thank you very much."

He decided to be open with her. "I guess you must have seen my towel when you came to my room the other time."

She wanted to shake her head and deny it, to save him from embarrassment but realized that would be a lie.

"Yes," she said, and quickly added, "but … that doesn't really matter. It's not as if it's so bad. I just thought I should buy a towel."

He smiled. "I could have bought these things but … you see, I have to share my salary with my younger ones."

"That's the right thing to do. I'm sure your parents are proud of you."

He shrugged. "Again, thanks."

After about a minute's silence, Ann spoke. "I want to ask you about something."

"Go ahead."

"What is your feeling about Daniel?"

"What do you mean?" He asked.

"What do you think of my relationship with him? I mean … what exactly is God's will about it? What will God want me to do? Mummie told me some things the other day and I know I shouldn't be in a relationship with a non-believer but ..." She shrugged. "I have some questions in my heart."

He took a deep breath before he spoke. "What do you think?"

"From what I now know, it's wrong to continue with him but I want to be very sure. I've been praying and thinking about it. I want your opinion before I make a final decision."

"To understand the will of God, let's try and answer some questions first. The answers will guide and make you know what God wants."

"Okay." She said, to indicate she was listening.

"The first question is, are you now a believer?"

"Yes." She answered without a moment's hesitation.

"Are you sure?"

"Yes." She repeated.

"Here's the second question. Is Daniel a believer?"

"I don't think so."

"What do you mean by you don't think so? From what you know about him and the way he lives, the things he does and the things he doesn't do, do you think he's a believer like you and me? Is his lifestyle in line with God's word? Does he believe what you believe about God?"

She took a deep breath as she considered those questions.

Daniel is not interested in church, he wants sex and he drinks beer especially when he is with his friends.

She shook her head slowly, "No, he is not a believer."

Sam took another deep breath. "If you know the truth, what will you do with it?"

"I'll obey."

"Okay. Let's search the Scriptures. Open the Bible to Second Corinthians chapter six, and read from verse fourteen."

Ann took her Bible and began to read, "Don't team up with those who are unbelievers. How can goodness be a partner with wickedness? How can light live with darkness? What harmony can there be between Christ and the Devil? How can a believer be a partner with an unbeliever? And what union can there be between God's temple and idols? For we are the temple of the living God. As God said: I will live in them and walk among them. I will be their God, and they will be my people."

Ann stopped and looked up at him.

"Continue." He said. "Read verses seventeen and eighteen."

"Therefore, come out from them and separate yourselves from them, says the Lord. Don't touch their filthy things, and I will welcome you. And I will be your Father, and you will be my sons and daughters, says the Lord Almighty."

She took a pen and underlined the verses.

He gave her one more Scripture and she read it as well.

Sam told her, "From these Scriptures, what do you think God's will is?"

"He doesn't want a believer to marry a non-believer." Ann answered.

"Also, let's look at the issue of premarital sex. Read First Corinthians chapter six, verse thirteen."

She opened to the chapter and began to read. "You say food is for the stomach and the stomach is for food. This is true, though someday God will do away with both of them. But our bodies were not made for sexual immorality. They were made for the Lord. And the Lord cares about our bodies."

Ann underlined it and looked up.

"Er, read from verse eighteen to twenty as well." He said.

She began, "Run away from sexual sin! No other sin so clearly affects the body as this one does. For sexual immorality is a sin against your own body. Or don't you know that your body is the temple of the Holy Spirit, who lives in you and was given to you by God? You do not belong to yourself, for God bought you with a high price. So, you must honor God with your body."

"Again, I'll ask you what you think God's will is, concerning premarital sex."

"He wants us to abstain." She answered.

"That's right. And where a person has been indulging in it, God wants the person to stop immediately. When a person has asked God for forgiveness and stopped having sex, God forgives the person. The slate is wiped clean and in His eyes, the person is a virgin. This is known as second virginity. In the physical sense, the person is not a virgin but as far as God is concerned, the person is. The Bible says if anyone is in Christ, he or she is a new creature, old things have passed away, behold all things have become new."

Ann nodded.

"So, His word is 'Come out from among them and be separate, and I will receive you.'"

Ann took a deep breath. "What if Daniel is willing to become a believer?"

"If he's willing to become a believer, that changes some things. In that case, both of you will need to pray to know if it's God's will for you to continue with the relationship. Also, all the wrong things you might have engaged in will have to stop. No sex until you marry. But most importantly, does God want you to marry that particular person? Is he the right man for you? Are you compatible? Those should be some of the questions where he is also a believer. But in Daniel's case, he is not yet a believer."

She sighed.

"Another thing that can guide you is your spirit because it is now regenerated. If you feel uneasy in your heart about it, that might be God telling you to stop and regain control of your life, to do something about the situation."

She nodded in understanding and said, "Thanks."

Guessing she still had questions in her heart, he asked, "Are there other questions?"

She sighed.

"Say whatever is on your mind." He encouraged her.

"If I'll be honest with you, I have two concerns."

As he listened to her, his gaze searched her face.

"Firstly, if I let Daniel go, when will I get another man? And secondly, the truth is that he's rich. Does it make sense to leave him?"

Sam nodded to show he knew what she meant. "I understand and I quite appreciate your honesty. Concerning these two issues, I'll give one answer. Trust in the Lord with all your heart and don't lean on your own understanding. In all your ways acknowledge Him and He will direct your path. God can and will do it for you, but you must be willing to obey and trust Him."

She drew a deep breath.

Now she had her answers. She would have to terminate her relationship with Daniel as difficult as that might be. It would be nice if she could bring him to church though, so he would be saved.

At home much later, Ann sat on her bed and began to think about Daniel. The right thing would be to let him go but ... those questions were still in her heart and she was bothered. Would she get another man? If yes, how soon would that be? Would she be able to get a man who would have money and also be a Christian?

As she weighed these questions in her heart, she prayed, asking God for help and direction. Then she took her Bible and began to search the Scriptures. She read the verses Sam gave her again, for a deep understanding of them. Then she turned her Bible to Luke chapter one and read verse thirty seven, "For nothing is impossible with God."

She stopped and considered the Scripture. God, does that mean You can give me a man who will be financially stable and a Christian? She knew the answer was yes. She sighed.

****

Throughout the week, Ann attended the lunch-hour fellowship and on Sunday, she worshipped at Sam's fellowship.

On Thursday evening, lying in bed, she called Kate's cell phone to know if she was back. When she said yes, Ann reminded her about going with her to church.

"Okay. I'll go with you. How do we meet?"

Ann did a quick thinking. "I'll come and pick you."

"Good. I'll expect you."

As soon as she ended the call, she phoned Sam.

****

Mid-week service had just ended and the executive members of Agape Campus Church were standing together, preparing to leave.

Sam switched his phone on and held it in his hand. About a minute after, it began to ring. It was the ringtone he had set for Ann.

Stepping aside, he picked it immediately, his heart racing in excitement, to his surprise.

"Hello Ann."

"Sam! I have good news for you!"

"Wow! I'm all ears. What is it? I can see you're excited." He said, smiling broadly.

"I am! I called Aunty Kate this evening. She's coming with me on Sunday for service!"

Sam was as excited as Ann had hoped he would be, and she was happy.

She went on, "We are coming together on Sunday."

"I'll expect you."

He returned to the others. "Hey everybody!"

They looked at him.

"Ann called me now. She's been talking to a lady and the lady is coming with her on Sunday."

"Wow!" Mummie exclaimed.

They were all happy.

Then Ade said, "There's something about Ann. I sense God's hand on her."

Mummie nodded. "She's coming up well. I'm surprised."

"You can't be as surprised as I am. You need to know how she used to dress. God has proved to me once again that there's no one He cannot change or use." Sam said.

He told them briefly of Ann's dream about talking to people about God.

"That may be God telling her He wants to use her." Ade said.

"That's what I told her." Sam said.

"She's a good lady. I pray she doesn't make a mistake in the area of marriage." Ade added.

"That has been part of my prayer for her." Sam revealed.

In bed much later, Sam was thinking about Ann. She had definitely changed and become a better person. In just about two months after her conversion, she was bringing someone to church. Interesting! He smiled.

It occurred to him that he was becoming very fond of her. He shook his head, not sure of how to deal with the feeling. It would be wrong to develop feelings for her. They were not at the same level. Such an attraction couldn't be from God and as such must be resisted by him. *Lord, help me! This has to stop!*

****

On Saturday, Ann told Mr. Noah she would like to use the BMW on Sunday as Kate would be going with her to church, and he agreed.

Sunday morning, she woke up early and began to get ready, wearing a gown that had a drawstring neck. Her high sandals had straps.

At 8am, she left in the BMW. Kate was having breakfast when she got there. She sat and waited patiently for her. At 9.30am, they left for Livingston University.

Praise and worship had begun when they got there. Sam saw them immediately and came out of the hall to meet them.

"Ann, how are you?" He asked with a smile, touching her shoulder briefly.

She answered and said, "Sam, I want you to meet Aunty Kate."

Sam greeted Kate, extending his hand to her, "I'm glad to meet you."

He led them inside and Ann sat beside Kate.

When first-timers were called, Kate stood up, along with six people. Ann was the first to welcome Kate. Some other people came, including Sam. He shook hands with Kate and tapped Ann on the shoulder in a friendly greeting.

Ann smiled.

They had a guest speaker, Pastor John. When altar call was made, Kate went out.

Ann was very happy.

After the service, Ade and Mummie came to them and invited Kate to go with them to the cafeteria for refreshment.

Kate looked at Ann.

Ann smiled, "That's what we usually do."

Kate shrugged.

Ann looked at Sam, "Will you drive?"

He collected the key, opened the car and they entered. They reached the cafeteria and got down.

The three ladies were told to sit while Sam and Ade went to get their meals.

They had started eating when a man came in.

"Joseph!" Sam called him.

Joseph looked back.

"What? Joseph?" Kate said under her breath.

Ann heard and looked at her. She saw that Kate looked shocked.

"Do you know him?"

"He's Jude's cousin!"

Ann kept quiet, hoping Kate would not begin to cry or do something silly.

Joseph came over. As he greeted them, his eyes fell on Kate.

"Kate?"

Kate stared at him.

"Do you two know each other?" Ade asked.

"Yes." Joseph answered.

Sam looked at Ann and saw she was looking at Kate with concern. *What's going on*?

"I didn't think it could be you when I saw you during the service. How are you?" Joseph asked Kate.

"I'm fine." She said briefly, pressing her lips together. She continued eating, realizing they were all looking at her.

"Do you care to join us?" Mummie asked Joseph.

"Sure. Er ... I'll just get my food." Joseph said and left.

"Are you okay?" Sam asked Kate.

She nodded.

"Ann?"

Ann looked at Sam and he raised his eyebrows in question.

She simply nodded.

Joseph returned and sat down.

"So, Joseph, how did you know her?" Ade asked.

All of them looked at him except Kate.

Joseph's eyes went to her first before answering the question. She concentrated on her food.

"Well, I'm her fiancé's cousin."

Kate looked up and responded hotly. "Ex-fiancé! I'm sure you know that!"

They looked at her.

Sam now understood. He whispered to Ade who nodded.

"Yes." Joseph agreed, looking at Kate. "I was shocked when I heard about it all. I'm sorry."

"Sorry? Why?"

"I mean ... I'm sorry for what happened. I almost couldn't believe it. I know -"

"Oh please!" She snapped. "Spare me that!"

"Aunty Kate," Ann called her quietly to calm her.

She shook her head at Ann. "No, let me express myself." She looked back at Joseph and said, "I don't need your pity. I've put it behind me. I've moved forward. I have decided to get close to God, I'm okay." Then stretching her hands out, she added, "You see? I'm fine!"

"I'm happy to hear that, and to see you here." Joseph said.

Ade cleared his throat and said, "Well, ladies and gentlemen, I'll suggest we continue eating. We can talk later."

"Yes, that's fine. Just one statement please." Joseph said, raising a finger up. He felt he needed to say something to encourage Kate to attend the New Believer's Class as she had just given her life to Jesus. He was the one in charge of the class and would have seven teachers under him for the seven classes involved.

"Okay." Ade said, looking at him.

Joseph looked at Kate with a corner of his mouth turned up in a smile. "I'm glad you came out to surrender your life to Jesus, Kate. That's the best decision anyone could make. God -"

"I'm glad too that I did." She interjected. "You should bring your cousin to do the same! He needs it. He cheated on me and ditched me!" Kate said, and then added, "And I hope you have made the decision yourself!"

Joseph looked as if he'd like to talk but Ade shook his head.

"Alright, let's eat."

When they finished eating, Joseph excused himself and left.

"Is he now a Christian?" Kate asked Sam.

"Yes. He is one of the good men we have in the fellowship."

Kate snorted.

"Okay, shall we go?" Ade said.

Outside, Ann and Kate entered their car and left.

"Did you have a good time there?" Ann asked Kate.

"I really did. Thanks for bringing me." Kate answered.

"But why did you behave that way to Joseph?"

"Why did I have to see him?"

Ann glanced briefly at her. "Of course, we didn't know we would see him there."

"What's he doing in that school anyway?"

They continued talking until they reached Kate's house and she got down.

****

On Friday, September 24, Ann was given an official car. She also collected her salary and set her tithe aside, to be paid on Sunday. She decided to buy a shirt for Sam.

She called Sam and told him about the car.

"That's good. What's the make and model?"

"It's a yellow Toyota Camry."

"Wow! That's great! I'll see it in the evening."

She also called Daniel to inform him.

In the evening, Ann was in her room when she heard her uncle's voice in the living room. Knowing Sam must be around, she came out of her room and greeted them. Sam handed the key over to Mr. Noah and said goodnight.

Ann quickly told her uncle she had been given an official car and asked if he would like to see it. He said he would see it the next morning as he was tired.

She told him she would want to show it to Sam. In the compound, after Sam had looked at the body of the car, Ann opened the door and Sam sat on the driver's seat. He prayed and thanked God for providing it for Ann.

On Sunday, Ann went to pick Kate for church again. After the service, Kate told her she would want to leave immediately.

"Okay. I just want to give something to Sam and then we'll leave."

While they stood aside, waiting for Sam who was praying with the executive members, Joseph came.

"Hello."

Kate began to walk away immediately. Ann followed, with Joseph behind her.

"Aunty Kate, wait!"

Kate stopped.

"You are now a Christian." Ann reasoned, almost in a whisper. "You have to be patient and control your emotions."

"I will be patient and control my emotions if he stays away from me!" She said, pointing at Joseph.

"What's the problem, Kate?" Joseph asked, looking confused. "Why are you behaving this way?"

Ann looked from one to the other, wishing Sam or Ade would come and save the situation.

"You are the problem!" Kate answered him.

"How?"

"You should leave me alone! I don't want to have anything to do with you or Jude, or any of your family members ever again in my life!"

Joseph responded, "You need to learn to take things easy. I haven't seen you in a long time, and I'm only trying to be nice and friendly ... to encourage you. I'm not the one who broke your heart, you know."

The last statement got Kate angrier. She was still thinking of a very rude comeback when she heard him say, "I haven't offended you in any way! I'm only trying to be help. Why should you turn your anger on me or the family as a whole?"

"Why not?" She threw at him.

He went on. "I heard about all that happened and what you almost did to yourself. How could I see you in my church and act as though I didn't know you?"

So, he was told that she wanted to kill herself, Kate thought as she glared at him. "Well, the family obviously has discussed me, and you've heard about all that happened to me. What else do you want to hear? What are you looking for?"

"Kate -"

"Joseph, stay away from me!" She snapped. "Just leave me alone! I don't want to have anything to do with any of you again! You, Jude, or one of your kind, alright?"

"One of my kind?" He repeated, and a corner of his mouth turned up in a smile. "What do you mean by that?"

When she didn't talk, he spoke again. "That's part of the problem! You have always been very stubborn! Stubborn and unnecessarily emotional. I hope there will be a change now that you're a Christian!"

Ann was shocked. She raised a hand to stop them. "Please -"

But Kate wasn't listening to her as she stared at Joseph. Did he just say she was stubborn and unnecessarily emotional?! Suddenly she was angry at Jude for breaking up with her and putting her in this situation. If Jude had not dumped her, Ann might not have needed to invite her to church, and she wouldn't have run into Joseph or be listening to his words. She could feel tears gathering in her eyes.

"Really?" She rapidly blinked to keep the tears back. "I've always been very stubborn and unnecessarily emotional?" She asked in disbelief. *Is he right? Is this why Jude left me, is this the reason I'm still single at thirty-one?*

"Yes! ... I mean, I'm only trying to encourage -"

"Really? Is that your opinion or what your family members told you? How have I been stubborn and unnecessarily emotional?" She asked as her mind went to the day Jude broke their engagement, how he said he no longer loved her, and that he had fallen in love with another lady. *What is wrong with me?* She wondered as tears began to roll down her cheeks.

"Aunty!" Ann called her.

"Oh, I'm sorry!" Joseph said and pulled her hand. "I didn't mean to upset you. I'm sorry."

Kate snatched her hand away and used a hand to cover her face. *Yes, I know that I can be stubborn and emotional, but I've been trying to work on myself,* she thought.

"Aunty, it's okay." Ann told her.

"I'm sorry." Joseph repeated.

She raised her head, glared at him and said, "What do you mean by saying sorry? How can you be sorry when you meant it? What exactly did you hear about me?"

Ann began to search her purse for tissue, but Joseph was faster. He produced his handkerchief and pressed it into Kate's hand.

She wasn't going to use it but seeing some people coming in their direction, she changed her mind. She cleaned her face and went on. "Is that what Jude told you? Is that my offense?"

Joseph frowned. "Jude? I -"

She added, "I asked him, but he didn't tell me what my offense was. He hurt me."

"I didn't discuss you with Jude. I haven't set my eyes on him for some time."

Kate wanted to leave but he took her hand to stop her. "I didn't mean what I said that way. I -"

"Okay, you can let go of my hand." She tried to free her hand. "I'm going to sit in the car."

"Alright." He released her hand.

As Ann and Kate walked toward the car, he followed them.

Opening the two front doors, Ann sat behind the wheel while Kate sat in the front passenger seat.

Joseph stood by her side.

Ann told him, "Er, Brother Joseph, why don't you go and leave her alone? You can see that she's upset. If you have something to say, you can say it later when she's ready to listen to you."

"I don't mean any harm." He told Ann with a slight smile, and then looking at Kate, he asked, "I ... do you want me to leave?"

"Yes, leave me alone!"

Just then, Sam, Mummie and Ade came.

"I've been looking for you." Sam said and then saw Joseph in the car. What's he doing here? He looked at Kate. "What's happening?"

Ann didn't talk."

Joseph greeted them and explained. "I just wanted to talk with Kate."

Sam looked at Ann.

Joseph told Kate, "Er ... Kate, can I have your phone number please?"

She didn't respond. What did he have to tell her?

He spoke again. "Can I get it from Ann?"

Ann looked at Kate and saw her nod.

"Okay. Thank you." Joseph said. Bringing out his phone, he flipped it open and asked Ann, "What's her number?"

Taking a deep breath, Ann checked her phone, and dictated it to him.

Joseph saved it, said goodbye, and left.

"Sam told me this is your official car." Ade said.

Ann nodded.

"Congratulations." He said.

"Congratulations." Mummie told her.

Ann thanked them.

"Let's pray on it." Ade said.

They did and some minutes after, Ade and Mummie went back to the other executive members.

Ann told Sam she had something for him but had to take Kate home.

"Maybe I'll see you next Sunday or thereabout." She said.

He checked his watch. "I can spare some time. I'll drive you home."

Ann was grateful.

♥ Chapter 6

Ann gave the key of her car to Sam. He opened the doors for them before sliding behind the wheel. On the way, Ann and Kate didn't talk much. When she was getting down, Ann told her she would come to her house the following day.

Back on the road, Ann told Sam what had happened between Joseph and Kate.

Then she said, "Tell me about Joseph."

"Well, this is about his third university. At the first two places, he was expelled for different malpractices."

Ann turned to look at him more closely.

He continued. "But shortly before he came here, he became a Christian, and he's been doing very well."

"Is he a good Christian?"

He nodded. "To the best of my knowledge, yes. We've never had any problem with him since he became a member of our fellowship. He could be very blunt and tough though, but he's okay. He's safe. He's a good guy.'

Ann laughed. "Those are the words I hoped to hear. I was a little scared when he shouted at Kate and she began to cry."

Sam laughed.

Ann unfastened her seatbelt and reached to the back seat to take the plastic bag containing the shirt. She gave it to Sam and he thanked her.

On her way from work on Monday, Ann stopped at Kate's house.

When Ann asked her about Joseph, Kate laughed.

Ann was surprised. That wasn't the reaction she had expected but she must admit this reaction was better.

"Don't mind him." Kate said with the wave of a hand.

"Tell me about him." Ann insisted.

"Well, I knew him before I knew Jude."

Wow! Ann's eyes widened.

"We were in the same university. That was Joseph's first university. He was a bad guy and because of that, I didn't want him. I preferred Jude and began to date him."

"Wow!" Ann exclaimed.

"When Joseph got to know, he was angry. At first, I feared for my life, but because Jude was involved, he simply stayed away. Soon after, he was expelled."

"Wow!" Ann exclaimed again. "Did you ever meet at family social functions at any time?"

"Er," Kate tried to remember, "we met about two times. We just greeted casually, and stayed away from each other."

"So, you must have been surprised to see him last week Sunday."

"I was."

"Wow! I don't know what to say." Ann said, laughing.

Smiling, Kate informed her, "He sent a text message to me last night, to apologize for the words he used."

"Did you reply?"

"No."

"Why?"

"I didn't want to." Kate shrugged. "Enough about me. Let's talk about you. Are you in a relationship with Sam?"

Ann laughed. "No. Why did you ask?"

"You are very close and seem to understand each other well."

Smiling, Ann explained, "Well, it may be because he's the person who invited me to the fellowship."

Kate considered the reply for some seconds before she said, "Somehow, you look like a couple together. You seem to fit. And looking at him, I think he really likes you. "

Ann laughed again. "We're just friends."

Some minutes after, Ann left.

On the way home, she received a call from Sam.

"Are you back at home?"

"No. I have just left Aunty Kate's place."

She told him what Kate had told her about Joseph.

"That's interesting." He said.

The next day, Tuesday, a man in his late twenties came to First Place Investment Company to discuss an investment on behalf of Airis Automobile Company where he worked. Ann had to attend to him and they exchanged business call cards. She looked at his card for his name and saw Fidelis.

When he began to make obvious passes at Ann, she decided to talk to him about God.

Fidelis laughed. "Someone had tried to convert me at a time but couldn't. I can allow a beautiful girl like you to convert me though, but I'll need to hear more." He said, getting up.

"When next are you coming here?" Ann asked.

"I don't know. If you really want to see me converted, come over. I'll listen to you."

Ann saw it as a challenge. If she could win him over and take him to church, that would be great.

"You can come to my house. We'll have more time to talk." Fidelis suggested.

"Okay, I will. You need to become a Christian. It will bring a change into your life. What's your address?"

He wrote it down for her.

"Will you be at home this Saturday?" Ann asked.

"What time?"

"Around 1pm."

Fidelis nodded. "I'll wait for you."

"I'll see you on Saturday. And I will be praying for you." Ann said.

She was happy. She had gone to Kate's house to talk to her and now, she was a Christian. If Fidelis would become a Christian as well, she would be happy.

It occurred to her to let Sam know she would be going to a man's house on Saturday to talk to him about God.

There's no need to tell him, she told herself. She would tell him after Fidelis had given his life to God. She would want it to be a surprise to Sam.

She began to pray for Fidelis.

On Saturday morning, her heart told her not to go to Fidelis' house but she brushed it aside. She could handle the situation. When she was ready to leave, she told Mrs. Noah, the only person at home, that she was going to a friend's house and would be back soon.

She left and drove to Fidelis' house. It was a self-contained apartment. Living alone, Fidelis opened the door, obviously happy to see her.

As Ann stepped inside, it suddenly occurred to her that she shouldn't have come alone. But she was already here and couldn't go back, she thought. Telling herself she would be okay, she shook off her fears. Besides, Fidelis looked like a good and gentle man.

"You look good." Fidelis told her. He wore a striped shirt on a pair of jeans. "Please have your seat."

"Thank you." Ann answered briefly.

"So, what do I offer you?"

She declined. She was there to preach, not to drink.

"So, have you thought about our discussion the other day?" She asked.

"No. I was waiting for you to come today, to continue." He walked over to the refrigerator in a corner, opened it and took a can of beer. He came to sit, opened the can and sipped.

Ann brought her Bible out and began to talk about the importance of salvation.

Eventually she stopped and asked him, "Are you willing to pray now?"

Fidelis answered, "I will, on one condition."

"What?"

"Have sex with me." He put the can in his hand down on a side table.

"What?" She smiled a little to hide her fear. "You know I can't."

"I thought you wanted to convert me."

"Yes but I can't do that." She pointed out, drawing in a steadying breath.

He sipped the beer again. Putting the can down, he said, "Then you're not serious about it."

She took her purse and got up.

He stood up and pulled her hand. "Where are you going?"

"I'm leaving." She said calmly, even though she was beginning to feel she might be in danger. "I've done what I came to do."

"No, you haven't." He drew her to himself and held her.

"No! Let me go!" Her voice rose in alarm.

"Not now!"

He pulled her dress up.

"No!" She pulled it down, and stepped back. "No! I'm not here for that! Be reasonable, Fidelis!"

"You don't need to play hard to get!"

"I'm not playing hard to get. I'm not interested. Period!" She walked quickly toward the door but he yanked her back.

She pulled her hand free and made for the door again but he blocked the exit, turning the lock. Pushing her roughly, he threw her on the sofa. As she tried to get up, he pushed her back, putting his knee on her tummy.

She screamed in pain.

He began to pull off his shirt.

Ann began to plead with him to let her go. "I just wanted to help you."

She was afraid. She hadn't told Sam where she was going. Nobody knew where she was. Jesus save me! She prayed.

He tossed the shirt aside and began to unbuckle his belt.

Suddenly there were voices by his door and then, a knock.

"Fidelis?"

"Oh, God!" He hissed.

"Please, let me go. Some people are here." Ann pleaded.

"Shut up!"

There was a louder knock. "Fidelis?"

He stood up.

Ann quickly got up and took her purse. She used a hand to smoothen her hair.

Fidelis went to the door and unlocked it.

Three men entered. They looked at Ann as she quickly walked past them before the door could close. She knew she must look a sight.

She heard the men say something to Fidelis and they laughed. As she started the car, she saw the curtain of Fidelis' window pull aside and two of the men looked out for her. She hoped none of them knew her. How would she explain her presence in Fidelis' apartment?

As she quickly drove out of the compound, she trembled. Her heart had told her not to go. She had not listened and had almost been raped.

Suddenly, she saw someone waving at her frantically. As she got close, she realized it was Sam. She stopped.

He opened the passenger door and entered, smiling broadly, obviously happy to see her.

"Where are you coming from?" He asked, fastening his seatbelt.

She didn't answer as she pulled back on the road. She didn't want him to see her tear-filled eyes.

"Where are you coming from?" He repeated, and looked at her, still smiling.

She didn't look alright. Looking closely, he saw that she was close to tears.

His smile faded and was replaced by a frown. "What is the matter?"

Tears began to roll down her cheeks. She wiped them off with the back of her right hand.

"Would you want me to drive?"

She slowed the car down and parked.

They got down and changed positions.

Pulling out, he asked, "Ann, what happened? Are you alright?"

She didn't talk.

"Talk to me please. Tell me what happened."

She began to weep. After a few minutes, she calmed down and told him all that happened.

He almost couldn't believe it. "Who is he?"

"He came to the office on Tuesday and I began to talk to him about God."

His eyes narrowed in shock. "A man came to your office just on Tuesday, and you went to his house, all alone!"

When she said nothing in response he spoke again, "Why didn't you tell me?"

Again, Ann was silent.

"Was that all that happened ... or did he actually rape you?"

"No, he didn't succeed."

"Are you sure you're okay?"

"Yes."

Sam was silent for some seconds as he drove on. Then he said, "I'm speechless, speechless and angry. I'm not sure of what to say. I'm upset, very upset."

There was silence again for some seconds before he continued, "We relate very well. You discuss various issues with me. Why didn't you tell me about this? Why didn't you tell me you were going to his house? I would have gone with you!"

Ann was still silent.

He went on, "You could have been raped or gang-raped. It could have even been worse! And no one would have known what happened to you. I doubt if you told your uncle or his wife where you were going. Or did you?"

She still didn't talk.

"You have suddenly become quiet. You went to a stranger's place without telling anyone. I'm angry, Ann."

Ann closed her eyes and took her lips in between her teeth. Sam had never spoken to her like this, and somehow, seeing him angry at her made her very sad.

"Ann?"

When there was still no response from her, he glanced at her and saw tears coming from her closed eyes.

Glancing back at the road, he took a deep breath. Maybe this was not the time to scold her. She had gone through an ordeal and would need to be comforted.

He took her left hand, "I'm sorry if my words seemed harsh." He paused before he spoke again. "Do you need to go to hospital?" He glanced at her.

She shook her head.

"Do you need anything?"

"No."

He released her hand.

"Are you going to your uncle's house or somewhere else?"

"My uncle's house."

"Alright."

But she was still very upset, and the way he had talked to her was very harsh. He wouldn't want her to leave feeling this way.

"I don't want you to leave yet. I'd want us to talk a little. Let's go to a place where we can talk and probably have something to drink."

"No."

"Let's go somewhere and talk. It will help you calm down. You have been crying. Going straight home with the way you look would make your uncle guess something happened to you."

"No. I want to go home."

"No, Ann -"

"Take me home!" She said angrily.

Sam was surprised. "Alright." He gave up and drove in the direction of Mr. Noah's house.

He would see her in church tomorrow. Then it occurred to him that because of what happened today and the way he talked to her, she might not want to come to church tomorrow.

He asked, "Will you be in church tomorrow?"

"Yes."

Good. "We'll talk tomorrow. We need to talk."

They reached Mr. Noah's house. Sam parked and left immediately.

Mr. Noah's car was not in sight which meant he was not back. Mrs. Noah was busy in her shop with two of her customers. Ann greeted her briefly. Olu was in the living room. She greeted him and went into her room.

She had a shower, changed her clothes and got in bed, thinking of what had almost happened to her. She found it difficult to believe what Fidelis had almost done. What would have happened if his friends had not arrived at the time they did? Or ... like Sam said, what if the friends had been interested in joining him in the evil act? She shuddered to think. That was a narrow escape, a miracle for her. It was God who saved her.

She began to thank God for rescuing her from danger. *Lord, You are faithful.*

****

In his room, Sam had a shower and got in bed, thinking about Ann. He was surprised at the way he reacted to the news of what almost happened to her. He hadn't been that angry in a long time. He suddenly realized that Ann had become his very close friend. If something bad had happened to her, it would have made him very sad. He was happy she escaped.

He continued to think of Ann. He remembered the way she looked when she was telling him about Fidelis, and the tears on her face. What if those men had messed her up? He would have to talk to her tomorrow, or probably talk to Mummie to warn all the ladies in the fellowship not to visit strangers or men they didn't trust.

He realized his feelings for Ann were stronger. Hissing, he reached out and took the remote control, pointed it at the TV and switched it on. He wanted some noise that would take his mind off Ann.

****

The next day, Sunday, Ann went to pick Kate for service. She noticed the lady was looking different, very beautiful. She had even fixed her hair and was looking radiant.

Ann commented on it.

"I've just bought the dress." Kate confessed. "Joseph may be seeing and talking with Jude. I don't want him to tell Jude that I'm looking miserable, wretched and sick. They need to know that I've moved on."

"That's good. That's the spirit." Ann said, smiling.

At Agape Campus Church, before the choir's special songs, Mummie came up and began to talk about rape and the dangers in ladies visiting strangers or men they didn't trust, alone. She also told ladies to be careful when trying to convert or do follow-up on men, saying it could be dangerous.

Ann was surprised at what she was hearing. Had Sam told Mummie of what had almost happened to her? She would see him after service and give him a piece of her mind!

Mummie went on, "According to statistics, rape by an acquaintance is the most common form of rape." She said and cited instances.

"Don't say you will convert him. Only God can do that. If a man you know needs to be talked to, involve a man you trust. Rape happens a lot but it can be prevented to a large extent. Read the book titled Rape & how to handle it."

When it was time for the message, Ade went forward. He started by announcing that there would be a special program on Saturday, the 16th of October tagged Love Feast at Ibrahim Dansuki Hall. It would start at 5pm and every member of the fellowship was expected to invite friends. He also said they would be having a guest minister on Sunday, 17th of October.

He prayed and began to preach.

After the service, Ann told Sam she needed to see him. He quickly left the others and went with her to stand by her car.

"Did you tell Mummie what happened yesterday?"

He shook his head. "No. Of course, I wouldn't. I only told her to warn the ladies about it. I didn't mention your name at all. Some other ladies might fall into the same error if not warned."

"Are you sure you didn't tell her it happened to me?"

He shook his head. "No. I'm not stupid."

"You're not stupid? Are you sure?"

"You know I'm not."

She laughed.

That made him happy. That meant she was back to her normal self.

"I was really scared yesterday when you told me about Fidelis. I've not been that upset in a long time." He confessed.

She smiled. "But I didn't get hurt."

"You could have been hurt, Ann." He pointed out, looking serious. "Don't let that happen again please."

She inhaled deeply. "Okay. You said yesterday that you'd like to talk to me."

"It's no longer necessary."

"In that case, I need to leave." She put a hand to her head.

"Are you alright?"

"I am. I just need to go and rest."

"Alright, give me some minutes." He said and went back inside.

Kate came to join Ann. While they were talking, Joseph came out of the hall, talking with a man. Shortly after, the man left and he strode toward Ann and Kate.

"Hello ladies."

Ann smiled and responded. Kate did not.

"Kate, can I see you for a minute?" He said.

"Look, Joseph, I'm not here because of you or anyone for that matter! If you're not going to stay away from me, I may have to stop attending this church altogether!"

Ann was shocked. *What's the matter with Aunty Kate*?

"No, you don't need to stay away." Joseph told her. "Don't worry, I will stay away. I'm sorry if I upset you." Then he added, "I never knew you disliked me so much."

With that, he turned, walked to a red car and drove off.

Sam returned. They talked briefly and soon, Ann and Kate left.

Much later, when they reached Kate's house, Ann got down with her. In the living room, she talked to Kate about her rude behavior to Joseph and her need to change now that she had become a Christian.

****

It was a Tuesday evening. As soon as lectures ended, Sam went to eight of the students and invited them to the Love Feast in his fellowship.

When he returned to his room, he invited Kofi and his friend too.

****

The next Sunday, after service, Ann and Kate saw Joseph coming with a lady. Ann knew he saw them but he walked past without looking in their direction. She didn't say anything to Kate, and Kate didn't bring it up.

Sam offered to drive them back.

On the way, he asked Kate if she would be coming for the Love Feast on Saturday.

"I don't think so. I have a wedding to attend that day."

"Ann, I'm sure you will attend." He said and glanced at her beside him.

"I'm not sure."

"Why?"

"I have a lot of things to catch up on, things to do."

"The program is at five in the evening. You have the whole day to do whatever you want to do, and at 4.30pm, you stop."

"I don't know. I'll see what I can do."

"I want you to come."

"Okay." She finally agreed.

On the Saturday, she attended the program and had a lot of fun.

Four of the people Sam invited turned up. Sam made sure they were comfortable. He made a mental note to call them the next day to appreciate them for coming for the program.

On Sunday, the guest speaker preached on 'God's kind of love'. At the end of his message, he asked the congregation to go around to greet one another, and that those who were not on talking terms should forgive and reconcile.

While Ann was wondering whom to go to, as she didn't have issues with any of the students, she heard Kate say 'excuse me'. She moved back and Kate passed.

Ann decided to meet some students whose names she didn't know. She introduced herself and asked for their names.

On her way back to her seat, Sam came to her with an outstretched hand. "Do we have anything against each other? If I've offended you in any way, I'd like to apologize now."

They laughed as they shook hands.

Soon after Ann returned to her seat, Kate came, looking pleased with herself.

"Who did you go to meet?" Ann asked in a whisper.

"Joseph." Kate answered, also in a whisper. She giggled.

Ann smiled. "So?"

Kate shrugged. "Well, I apologized. That was all."

****

On Tuesday, Daniel returned from Warri and came to Mr. Noah's house in the evening.

Ann had just returned from work.

He hugged and tried to kiss her but she pushed at his chest and stepped back, her heart racing. The time of decision had come. She would have to end the relationship now.

"When did you return?" She asked instead.

"I came this morning."

"Please sit down."

He did, putting his cell phone and a small plastic bag in his hand on the side table nearest to him.

"Good to see you. What do I offer you?"

"You're all I want, right now."

She smiled. "I'm sorry but I'm not on the menu."

"Pity."

"So, do you want something to eat?"

"Yes but first things first. I've missed you. Can we go away this weekend?"

"Daniel, be serious."

"I am. You want to know how serious I am?" He stood and tried to grab her.

She ran away, laughing. "I will scream if you touch me."

"Go ahead. Your uncle won't send me out. He knows we are in a relationship. You're more or less my wife."

"I'm not your wife. We are not married. You have not even proposed to me."

He laughed as he sat down. "I don't think I want to eat. Just give me something to drink."

She left and soon returned with a can of juice and a glass cup on a tray.

"So, how have you been?" He asked her.

"I've been doing well. And you?"

"I'm fine. Did you miss me?"

Ann sighed and looked at him. She had to tell him about God and also end their relationship now. She would start with church matter first.

Taking a deep breath, she blurted out, "As I've told you, I've been attending Sam's church."

"Sam's church?" Daniel asked incredulously. "I asked if you missed me, you said you have been attending Sam's church. Have you been seeing him?"

"That's what I'm explaining. I've been going to his church."

"Why his church? For what?"

"But I told you I've been going to church."

"Yes, you did but you didn't tell me it was Sam's church."

"Well, I've been going to church and I've become a Christian."

What she said didn't seem to make any difference to him as he said, "That's fine, but I think you should stay away from Sam. He's a driver and a student. Why his church? What were you thinking?"

"Daniel, there's nothing. He's not that kind of person."

"I don't know what kind of person he is."

"He's a Christian." She said. "Can we go to the church together on Sunday?"

"Why do you talk like this? Just listen to yourself. If at all I will go to church, why should it be Sam's church?"

"Okay, I'm sorry. That was actually thoughtless of me. Which church would you like to attend?"

"Well, you know my opinion about such things."

"Yes and you too know what my opinion was but things have changed with me."

"And because things have changed with you, things must change with me?"

Now, the time had come to terminate their relationship. "Daniel -"

"Look, I'm not here for that!" He stood and walked to stand by the window. "I don't want any form of argument. I've been under a considerable amount of pressure, trying to take care of my dad, encourage my mother, and at the same time, run the businesses among other things."

She had forgotten to ask how his father was!

He continued. "With the way things are, we may have to fly him abroad."

"What are the doctors saying?"

He shrugged. "They are treating him but my mother thinks we should take him abroad. The whole thing was getting too much for me. I needed a break and that was why I came to Lagos to see you. I need some peace but it appears I'm in the wrong place."

That almost broke her heart and resolve as she said, "Oh, Daniel,"

He used a hand to touch his head. "My head is pounding right now."

"Oh, I'm sorry."

He returned to his seat and finished his drink.

"I'll suggest you go home and rest." She said.

"That's what I have to do. I'll be going to Abuja by next week."

"What are you going to do?"

"My dad has an office there and ... there have been some challenges for some time. Due to his ill health, he has not been able to go to resolve the issues."

Ann sighed. She might have to wait for a better time to end the relationship. He seemed to have enough stress right now.

"Any idea when you'll be back in Lagos?"

"I'm not sure." He answered, taking his cell phone and the plastic bag.

He stood and offered her the plastic bag. "This is for you."

"A gift?"

"Yes, a watch and the handset you asked for."

She was supposed to terminate the relationship but here he was, offering her a wristwatch and a handset. She didn't know what to say.

She eventually found her voice and said, "I don't think I should accept them."

"Why?

She wanted to say 'Because the relationship is over. I can't see you again,' but she simply shook her head.

"It's a gift. It doesn't matter if things don't work out between us." He put the plastic bag on the table and walked toward the door.

He stopped. "If you're going to church on Sunday, I think you should try another church, instead of that same place."

"Why?"

"You should see what's going on in another church. It makes sense." He looked at her as if he thought her question was stupid.

As she saw him off to the white car he brought, she thanked him for the gifts.

In her room, Ann flung herself on the bed. "Lord, help me! I want to please You! I should have told Daniel that I would not be seeing him again but I developed cold feet at the last minute. I'm sorry. But Lord, will I get another man, a Christian, who is like him if I let him go?"

She began to weep.

When she had calmed down, she took her Bible to read. Then it occurred to her that for as long as she held on to those questions giving her doubts, she would not do the right thing. She must let those questions and doubts go, and trust God with her life.

Realizing her error, she determined she would end their relationship the next time he came to Lagos. The truth was that they were now completely two different people. If she remained with him, she could not please God.

And regarding his suggestion about church, she might attend the church in the neighborhood on Sunday.

She called Sam and told him Daniel had come to see her. She had planned to end their relationship but had not followed it through.

"I feel upset, I feel that I let God down." She said.

"Well, the important things are to continue to move forward and make sure you obey God. If you do something wrong, ask for forgiveness and move on, don't stop." He told her.

"Thanks.'

She informed him of her plan to attend another church on Sunday.

"Is there a particular reason you want to attend another church?"

She didn't want to mention Daniel so she said, "I just want to worship in another church and see what's going on there."

"Are you going with Kate?"

"I will call her now and ask if she's interested."

Ann called Kate and Kate told her there was a church in her neighborhood she could attend too.

"Which church is that? What's the name?"

"The Restorer's Tabernacle."

"Okay. We'll compare notes afterwards."

The next day, Sam sent a text to her.

The place you start is not as important as the place you finish. Keep going, don't look back. I'm proud of you.

On Sunday, Ann went to the church in her neighborhood. The service was good but she found she preferred Agape Campus Church.

Later in the day, Sam called her.

"So, how was service?"

"It was okay but I think I prefer your church."

He laughed. "Why?"

"Perhaps because I'm already used to your fellowship but somehow, I couldn't flow in the church I attended this morning."

He laughed. "Well, we all missed you. Some of the people asked after you."

They continued talking.

 # Chapter 7

On Saturday afternoon, Sam phoned Ann and told her, "I have resigned from Best Insurance Company."

Surprised, she asked, "Why? Did something happen?"

"No. I'd like to get another job."

"You don't have one yet?"

"No."

"Then you shouldn't have resigned." Ann told him.

"The right thing to do is get another before you leave one."

"I know but I just felt I should resign. I worked four and a half years there as a driver. I need something different."

"Oh, I see. But you didn't tell me about it at any time."

"I know. I'd been considering it for some time but finally decided on Friday morning."

"And what did my uncle say?"

"Not much. When he asked me, I simply told him that I felt it was time for me to leave."

"Oh I see." She said, then added, "I don't know why but I think you should have told me about it."

"That's true. I'm sorry."

"That's okay. I mean, it should be your decision. How will you now cope financially?"

"I'll manage. I'll survive." He said and laughed.

The next day, she went to Sam's church with Kate. After service, they saw Joseph and he greeted them warmly.

****

It was 11.30am on Monday. Ann had just returned to the office from a company and was immersed in writing a report when her cell phone began to ring. It was Sam calling to say hello.

She told him she would be going to Ibadan on official duty on Thursday. She had to meet with some people at a company.

"Are you going by public transport?"

"No, I'm going in my car." Ann answered.

"Are you going alone or going with some people?"

"It's only me. I intend to leave by 9am."

"Er, do you mind if I go with you?" Sam asked.

"You'd like to go?"

"I can, that is if you want. I'm free that day. I'll drive."

She liked the idea. "I don't mind. In that case, let's meet at your school gate on Thursday by 9am."

"It's okay by me."

A little after twelve, while working on the computer, the receptionist called Ann on the intercom to inform her of the presence of Pastor Emma.

Pastor Emma?

"Let him come in."

Soon, he was in her office. He wore an expensive looking dark suit.

"Please sit down. This is a surprise."

Smiling he said, "I hope it's a pleasant one."

"Sure. How has your day been?"

They continued talking.

"Will you be going for the lunch-hour fellowship so we can go together?"

"I will." Ann replied and glanced at her watch. The time was 12.35pm.

Ten minutes after, they left with James for the fellowship. On the way, Pastor Emma was talking with Ann.

"Can we have lunch together tomorrow, probably after the fellowship?"

Ann smiled. Recently, she had been having the feeling that God was calling her to serve in the ministry in one capacity or the other, and that she would marry a pastor. And here was a pastor, who worked in a bank! She looked at him briefly. He wasn't bad looking. Could he be the right man for her?

It should be safe to have lunch with him at a restaurant, more so because he was a pastor.

She shrugged. "That's fine."

"Will after the fellowship work with you?"

"Yes." She said.

"That's good. I'll look forward to it."

****

After the fellowship the next day, Ann and Pastor Emma went to a restaurant not too far from their offices.

As they ate, they talked, trying to get acquainted with each other.

"So, when did you become a Christian?" He asked her and she told him.

Ann looked at him, studying him.

She asked about his church and what he did there.

"I'm the Youth Pastor." He said and told her what his responsibilities were. "It would be nice if you would worship in my church one of these days."

He brought his call card out and wrote the name and the address of his church at the back. As Ann collected it, she made him know she wasn't making any promise about coming.

"I'd like to visit you at home, away from office. Can I have your address?"

She was hesitant. "Er, your best bet is to come to the office. It may be difficult to get me at home."

"That's a lady's excuse to put off a man. Are you trying to avoid me?" His gaze held hers.

She laughed. He smiled.

"Can I have your address, please?"

She was still reluctant.

"I'd like the opportunity to get to know you better, Ann. I like you. We can't have much time in the office, and due to the nature of my job, I close late." He explained.

"Please."

"Alright." She wrote her address for him.

"I'll let you know when I'm coming."

"Please do."

At home in the evening, she began to pray about Pastor Emma. God reveal who he is to me.

****

On Thursday, Ann got to the campus gate at 9.14am and found Sam already there. He had a baseball cap on. She got down, gave him the keys and went to the passenger side.

He slid in. As he adjusted the seat, he told her, "I got to the gate at 8.30am."

She smiled. "Why?"

"I wanted to ensure I didn't keep you waiting." He adjusted the mirror as well and hooked the seatbelt.

"It seems it's going to rain. The sky is getting dark." Ann observed.

"I think so too. It's a good thing I'm with you to drive." Sam said.

Some minutes after, it began to rain and Sam turned on the wipers.

When the rain became heavier, Ann asked him to drive slowly as the ground was wet.

Halfway to Ibadan, the rain stopped. They reached Ibadan at about 10.30am and drove straight to the company where Ann was to have the meeting. Sam parked the car in the company's compound.

As Ann was getting down, he told her, "Call me when you're through."

"I will." She said and walked into the building.

Sam locked the doors of the car and walked out of the compound. Outside, he saw a large bookshop on the other side of the road. He crossed the road and went into the bookshop. He spent close to an hour there, checking many books and CDs. He kept his phone in his hand so he would quickly know when Ann called.

Thereafter, he left the bookshop and went into a supermarket that was some blocks away. After about thirty minutes, he returned to the office and sat at the reception to wait for Ann. He watched CNN news on the flatscreen TV placed in a corner.

At about 1.30pm, his phone began to ring. It was Ann. Picking it immediately, he said, "Hello Ann."

"Where are you?"

He was about to answer when he saw her step into the reception with the phone to her ear.

She saw him and smiled. "Oh you're here." She ended the call.

He stood. "Are you through?"

"Yes."

They said goodbye to the receptionist and left. In the car, Ann asked him, "So, what did you do to occupy yourself while waiting for me?"

He told her the places he visited. Then he asked, "How did the meeting go?"

"It was okay." She told him about it. Then she said, "I'm hungry. I didn't know it was going to take so long."

"I saw a restaurant on my way to the supermarket. Would you want us to go there?"

"Yes. I hope it won't be very expensive." She said, smiling.

"I hope so too."

Soon, he was parking the car in front of the restaurant. They entered and sat in one of the booths. A waiter brought the menu to them. Looking at it, they found the prices were reasonable and they ordered their meals.

As they ate, they talked. Sam kept his eyes on her as he listened to her words.

"So, when is your birthday?" He asked her.

"It's next month." She told him.

"What's your plan? Are you inviting friends over?"

"I haven't made any plan. I haven't given it a thought."

He didn't say anything.

"Now that you've mentioned it, I may celebrate it in a small way. I'll invite some few friends over." She told him.

"Well, let me know if there's anything you'll want me to assist you with."

"Okay. Thanks."

About thirty minutes after, they were in the car, on their way back to Lagos and they spent the time in easy conversation.

In bed at night, Sam could not sleep as he thought about Ann. He had many questions flying around in his head.

Was he falling in love with her? If that was the case, would she be interested in a relationship with a starter like him, someone just coming up in life, who had little or nothing to offer her? He didn't have money, let alone a car!

Was this attraction one sided? He stopped to consider this question. She usually asked for his opinion on issues and she was free with him. They discussed freely and he could say they were good friends. But did she feel anything for him? Would she want their relationship to go beyond friendship? How should he handle his feelings? And what was God's will concerning this?

****

On Sunday, Ann was back at Agape Campus Church with Kate. After the service, Kate told her she would like to leave as soon as possible as she would need to do some work at home.

"Okay, when Sam gets here, we can leave." Ann said.
"Fine."

Ann asked her, "What changes have you noticed in your life since you became a Christian?"

Kate smiled and answered, "Well, I feel at peace and ... I'm happy. I feel different somehow, I can't really explain it."

Ann nodded in understanding, having felt the same way when she newly became a Christian.

Kate went on, "With what I now know about God, I believe I can better handle issues of life and whatever may come my way. I know God is with me."

"I'm happy to hear this."

"Another thing, I used to be afraid of darkness and being alone but now, I'm no longer afraid."

"Wow!" Ann exclaimed joyfully. "That's great! I think people need to hear this."

Kate smiled. "My opinion about Christians and Christianity has changed as well. I used to wonder 'what are these people doing?' But now I understand. All I want to do is please God."

"Aunty Kate," Ann began.

She saw Joseph coming and stopped.

After greeting both of them, he concentrated on Kate.

"So, how have you been?"

"I've been good." Kate replied with a big smile.

Ann moved away a little.

About ten minutes after, Kate came to her.

"He said he will take me to my house." She informed Ann.

"Take you home?"

"Yes." Kate answered, giggling.

"That's fine. Maybe I should mention it to Sam."

"Okay."

Ann went to meet Sam who was with the executive members.

When he saw her, he took an excuse, stood up and came to her.

Ann quickly told him that Joseph had volunteered to take Kate home, and he said it was okay.

Ann went back to Kate, and soon, Kate and Joseph left.

Some minutes after, Ade, Mummie and Sylvester went with Ann and Sam to Sam's room. While they were all talking, Ann took a sheet of paper from her purse, and wrote on it.

Do I tell them about my birthday?

She gave it to Sam. He read it and nodded.

As soon as there was a pause in their discussions, Ann spoke, "My birthday is coming up on December 10, which is a Friday. I'll want to mark it in a small way in my house and I want us to plan it together. So, can we discuss it?"

"That's Mummie's job." Sylvester said.

Mummie sat up. "Did you say December?"

"Yes. 10th of December but the celebration will be on Saturday, the following day."

"That's about five weeks away. It's a good thing you brought it up now because it will require good planning. We'll need to write some things down so we don't forget." Mummie suggested.

Ann glanced at Sam. "I'll need a sheet of paper."

"I'll need one too." Mummie said.

Sam tore some sheets from his jotter on the table.

"First, about how many people are we looking at?" Mummie asked.

"Between sixty and seventy, I think." Ann replied.

Mummie wrote on her paper.

Ann too wrote on her paper.

Mummie looked up. "Which will it be, snacks or food?"

"Food. I can get a caterer to handle it." Ann said.

"Well, except you really want a caterer to handle it, I can get some of our sisters in the fellowship to do the cooking. They cook well, and they'd gladly do it. That will save you some money. We'll only need to get plates and cutleries."

"Getting plates and cutleries won't be a problem. Between my mother and my uncle's wife, I'm sure I will get enough. But are you certain you'll get sisters who can do the cooking, and they will do it well?"

Mummie chuckled. "Yes." She mentioned four names. "They will do it, and do it well too."

Ann glanced at Sam for his approval.

He smiled and nodded. "They are good. They will gladly do it. You don't need to worry about it. Consider it done if it's coming from Mummie."

Ann relaxed. If Sam told her it would be done, she believed it would be done. She trusted his judgment. If he had to do the cooking by himself, he would, to make sure it was done!

"Okay. How much will we need to cater for about one hundred people?"

"One hundred people? I thought you said between sixty and seventy?" Sam asked.

"It's better to have surplus food than for it not to be enough. Whatever remains could be kept in the refrigerator." Mummie said. "I'll discuss with the sisters. They will give us an estimate of the total cost."

"Where will they do the cooking?" Ann wanted to know.

"They can come over to your house, if it's okay."

"Yes but, are you very sure they will come?" Ann asked.

Sam laughed. "If Mummie asks them to come, they will. It will be done."

"Okay. Thanks." Ann said.

"What about drinks and water?" Ade asked.

"I'll get them from my uncle's wife."

Mummie looked at Sam. "Arrange for some of the men in the fellowship to handle it that day."

Sam nodded.

"We'll need to get tables and chairs." Mummie went on.

"We can get them from a place not too far from my house." Ann said. "How many of them?"

Mummie told her.

"We will need linen cloths or whatever we can get to cover the tables. It will also be nice if we can get flowers and vases to decorate the tables, especially the high table where the celebrant and her family members will be seated." Mummie said.

Ann wrote them down.

"What else?" Mummie asked and looked at the men.

Sylvester spoke. "Are you printing invitation cards?"

Ann shook her head. "No. I will call to inform the people I'm inviting."

"In that case, you will need to remind them by calling them again or sending a text message when it's about a week or four days to the day." Ade said.

Ann agreed.

Ade suggested that Sam should give the word of exhortation but he declined.

"I can't. I'll need to help her with whatever needs to be done on that day."

"That's true. In that case, I'll take it. Or better still, we can invite Pastor John." Ade said.

"Ah, that's good." Ann said. Pastor John was a good preacher.

"I almost forgot about decorations." Mummie said.

About an hour after, they had agreed on the plans. Ann got up and they escorted her to her car.

****

When Sam returned to his room, Kofi asked, "Has your girlfriend gone?"

Sam laughed a little, "Who?"

"Your girlfriend. That fair-skinned lady."

Sam laughed again. "I don't know what you're talking about."

Kofi snorted. "Stop deceiving yourself. You Christians pretend a lot."

Sam laughed again. "But she's not my girlfriend. Maybe you don't even realize she's not a student."

"I know she's not a student. People have told me."

"You've been discussing us?" Sam asked in surprise.

Kofi laughed.

Sam frowned. "I don't like it. And I don't think Ann would appreciate it as well, more so because it's not true. You know how rumors spread."

"Okay. I understand but tell me the truth, you like that girl?"

"Of course, I like her. She's a Christian sister."

One of Kofi's friends entered the room.

Kofi told his friend, "I've been asking Sam about that fair lady."

"The one who brings the yellow car?"

Sam laughed.

The friend smiled, "Sam knows a good thing. He's not like some Christians who don't know anything except the blood of Jesus."

The three of them laughed.

Grinning broadly, Sam said, "Look, leave me alone. I've told you she's just a friend."

****

In her room much later, Ann called Daniel and told him she wanted to mark her birthday. She hoped he would be there, so he could hear the sermon and become a Christian.

"Where are you now?" She asked.

"I'm still in Abuja but I'll leave next week to return to Warri."

"Do you think you can come for it? It's in December."

"Well, I'm not sure yet."

"Does that mean you will miss it?"

"You know what? On second thought, I'll tell one of my friends. If he's willing to drive down with me, then you'll see me."

"Let me know on time if you'll be coming, please."

Some hours after, he called her back. "My friend won't be free that weekend. He has to be at work."

"You should be able to do something about it, Daniel. Don't you have some other friends you can tell? I don't want you to miss it."

"My other friends won't want to come. I'm sorry. I'll be around toward the end of December."

"Alright."

At about 6pm, her phone rang. It was Pastor Emma.

"I'm in your neighborhood. Are you at home?"

"Yes."

"Do you mind if I check you up?"

"That's okay." Ann replied.

"Very well. I'll be at your place soon."

Ann quickly got up, put on a nice dress and applied powder to her face.

When Pastor Emma arrived, Mr. and Mrs. Noah were in the living room. Ann introduced Pastor Emma to them.

Shortly after, the couple discreetly left the living room and went to the balcony.

Ann gave Pastor Emma juice to drink. She told him about her birthday and he promised to come.

After he had left, Mr. Noah asked Ann about him.

"He works in a bank."

"Which bank?"

She told him.

"That's good. Come to think of it, I've not been seeing Daniel. Why?"

Ann told him that Daniel's father had been ill and Daniel had had to run his businesses for him.

****

The following Sunday, Kate told Ann she would attend the church in her neighborhood.

Later in the evening, she called Ann.

"I've decided to be worshipping in the church."

Ann was surprised. "Why?"

"You can't be coming every Sunday to pick me. For how long would we do that?"

"But I don't mind."

"No. There's no need. I've discussed with Joseph and he has promised to bring me to Agape, whenever he can."

"Is that what you really want?"

"Yes."

"Okay, that's fine."

****

On the third Sunday of November, while Sam and Ann were in the cafeteria after the service, Sam's cell phone alerted him of a text message. He took his phone and opened the message.

He suddenly laughed.

Ann looked at him, wondering what was so funny.

He moved his chair to her side, and placing his arm along the back of her chair, he gave her his phone. "Read this."

Ann began to read the message.

Dear Brother Sam, I have been praying and thinking about this for some time but I realize it has to be done. I believe you are my husband. God has convinced me about it. Please don't disobey - Sister Agnes.

As Ann read it, she smiled. She eventually turned to look at Sam and found that their faces were very close. He seemed to realize this as he removed his hand from the back of her chair and moved back.

Ann smiled. "This is a big one. Do I know her?"

"No. She's my coursemate."

"So, what do you think?"

"That's not true, of course. There's nothing like that."

"Why?"

"Sister Agnes?" He asked with a frown. "No way! We are not compatible in any way. I don't even know her that much, we just relate casually. If I'd sat down to talk with her, it couldn't have been more than twice. I invited her for the love feast and she came. That was all."

"So, what will you do about it?"

"I will see her tomorrow and talk with her. It's her emotion that's talking, not God."

"Are you sure?"

"Positive. There's a way God works. There should be a level of attraction. And if God was involved, Agnes should wait for God to talk to me after which I would propose to her, not the other way round."

Ann smiled. "Tell me, what kind of a lady will you want to marry?"

He laughed. "Well, some years back, I had it in mind that she must be tall, slim, dark in complexion and wear glasses."

"Wear glasses?" She asked incredulously. "What has that got to do with marriage?"

They laughed.

"As I said, that was years back before I became a strong Christian. All that has changed now. What really matters to me now is that she must be beautiful inside and outside. I'm going to be a pastor, so she must want to work for God as well, I mean, be in the ministry with me."

"What if she doesn't want to be in the ministry?"

"The person I'm going to marry must love to be in the ministry. I will have put all that into consideration before proposing to her. We can't have a good marriage if as a pastor's wife she doesn't want to be in the ministry. She may not necessarily stand behind the pulpit to preach but she must be willing to support me. Of course, as a pastor's wife, there will be times when she will have to be in front to encourage the congregation."

Ann nodded. "That's true. I also feel strongly called to the ministry. The man I'm going to marry must want to be in the ministry as well."

Really? Suddenly looking serious, he leaned forward and asked, "What do you feel called to do?"

"I love to talk to people about God, counsel and pray for them."

"That's a pastoral work."

She shrugged. "I think so."

"Wow! That's incredible. Some people have been Christians for long but still don't know what they are called to do. Some don't even want to do anything. You became a Christian in July and already you're talking about your calling."

God, is she the one for me? He asked silently, looking at her intently.

"Pastor Emma has been getting in touch with me." She blurted out.

He frowned. "The one who attends the lunch-hour fellowship and works in a bank?"

"Yes."

His frown deepened. "Why is he getting in touch?"

She smiled. "He said he likes me."

He stared at her, trying to know what was on her mind. Was she falling in love with Pastor Emma?

"Are you falling in love with him?"

She laughed. "Love? So soon? No. God hasn't told me anything about him."

"How would you know who the right man is?"

She looked at him as if she considered that question unnecessary. "I'm a child of God. God will talk to me."

He asked another question. "What things are you looking for in a man, what are the things that matter to you?"

"The man must love God, love me and be of good character."

He probed further, feeling his way along. "Have you met anyone?"

She laughed. "Wait and see."

"No, I want to know now." He insisted.

"Sam, wait and see. I will definitely tell you about it when the time comes." She said and laughed.

Releasing a long sigh, he prayed silently, *Lord, I didn't ask to develop feelings for her. How am I supposed to handle these feelings?*

The next day, after praying for wisdom to tackle Agnes, Sam left his room for lectures. Agnes was present. When the lectures ended at 8pm, Sam quickly called her.

Agnes was very slender, tall and dark in complexion.

They stood aside while other students were talking.

"I got your text message but I'm not sure I quite understand." Sam said.

"The message was clear."

"Yes but I mean ... what gave you the idea? How did God talk to you or what got you convinced that I'm the right man for you?"

Agnes shifted from one leg to the other.

"Oh I'm sorry. Would you like to sit down?"

"Yes." She said.

Sam drew two chairs and they sat down.

"So, how are you sure I'm the man for you?"

"Well, Brother Sam, I want to make it clear to you that I wasn't thinking of you before this time. I was simply praying that God should reveal my husband to me. Then last month, I told God to make the Christian man for me get in touch with me and ask me out. That was on Sunday, and on Tuesday, you came to me after lecture and invited me to the love feast in your fellowship."

Sam laughed.

"Please don't laugh. This is serious."

He tried to control his laughter. "I'm sorry. Please go on."

She did. "I too found it difficult to believe. I thought it was just a coincidence. I attended the program and afterwards, I asked God to confirm His will by making you call me on phone."

Oh my God! Sam almost couldn't believe what he was hearing.

"And you called me on phone."

"I called to thank you for attending the love feast!"

"It was an answer to my prayer." She insisted.

"This is unbelievable!" Sam exclaimed, looking down.

"What is unbelievable?"

He looked up. Did he say that aloud?

Clearing his throat, he said, "So, you put out a fleece to know who the man for you was?"

"Yes."

"But Agnes -"

"Sister Agnes." She corrected him.

He laughed.

"What's funny?"

Raising his hands up in apology, he said, "I'm sorry."

He continued laughing while Agnes waited for him.

When his laughter subsided, he said, "I won't laugh again, it's a promise. Now, Ag - Sister Agnes, putting out a fleece like Gideon did is not a reliable way of knowing

God's will, and you should have known that by now. It's unfortunate that some Christians still practice this."

"Brother Sam, God granted Gideon his requests. He gave him the signs he asked for."

"I know but that still didn't mean it was the right thing to do. The fact that Gideon did it and he got an answer did not mean it was acceptable to God or that it was a good idea. Abraham and Isaac lied when they were asked about their wives. God did not kill them for it but we all know they lied and what they did was wrong."

"That was different." Agnes argued.

"It wasn't."

"It was." She insisted. "In Gideon's case, he only wanted to be sure of what God would do."

"He didn't need to ask for signs. God had already told him he would be with him and he would defeat the Midianites. Why did he ask for signs again? That did not show a strong faith, that was a weak faith. And in the book of Matthew, Jesus condemned the practice of asking for signs. We are to walk by faith and not by sight or putting out a fleece. And as many as are led by the Spirit of God are the children of God."

Agnes looked a little confused. "But Brother Sam, I've put out a fleece a number of times, asking for particular signs and it worked for me."

"It might have worked for you but that did not mean it's the best idea or that it's approved by God. It's not a mature faith. Putting out a fleece contradicts the Biblical teachings on faith. In fact, it's a dangerous way of determining the will of God. God may allow it for a new believer but He expects the person to grow up spiritually and pray properly."

Agnes sighed, and looked as if she had realized her error.

They continued to talk.

Then Sam said, "I am definitely not God's will for you, Sister Agnes. But don't worry, keep on praying and I'll be praying for you as well. The right man will come, I'm sure. You're a good person."

She smiled a little, "I'm glad you think so. And I'm sorry if I embarrassed you in any way."

He denied it immediately. "You did not embarrass me. And we are still friends. I'll be praying for you."

****

After service on Sunday, Ann asked Sam if he had seen Agnes.

He laughed. "Yes. I've seen her."

Smiling she said, "So, what did she say?"

"She put out a fleece and concluded that I must be the right man for her."

Ann frowned slightly. "What do you mean by 'She put out a fleece?'"

He explained, "The phrase 'put out a fleece' is from the story of Gideon in the Bible. God told Gideon to go and defeat the Midianites. Then Gideon asked God for a sign. He asked God to make a fleece of wool wet with dew on one morning, then totally dry on the following morning, as a sign that God would definitely deliver Israel from the Midianites."

Ann had heard the story before but had not read it herself. She asked him where she could find the story in the Bible.

Sam told her and went on, "When a person who is considering whether or not to embark on a journey says,

'Lord, if it rains today, then I'll know you want me to travel tomorrow,' or in trying to choose between two men, a woman says, 'Let the right man between the two send a phone card to me today', that's putting out a fleece."

Ann smiled and shook her head. "That's not the right thing to do. I'm just about five months old in the faith but I know that sort of thing can't be right."

"Some Christians do it." Sam said.

"Was that what Agnes did?"

Sam nodded and explained to her everything Agnes told him.

Ann began to laugh until tears came from her eyes. "Are you serious?"

Sam was also laughing. "Yes."

"Oh my God! This is hilarious!"

When their laughter subsided, she asked, "So, what did you tell her?"

Sam told her what he said to Agnes.

"Wow! You handled that well." She gave him a pat on the shoulder.

"Thanks."

Shortly after, Ann entered her car and left. Sam went back to meet the other executive members.

Ade told them, "I went to Penny Books yesterday. The owner told me she needs someone to supervise the bookshop."

Sam had met the owner a number of times at the bookshop. The woman who lost her husband in February was in her late thirties.

"To supervise the bookshop? I'm interested." Sam said immediately.

"She gave me her phone number." Ade said, bringing his cell phone out. He scrolled down to Penny Books.

"Here it is."

He dictated the number and Sam saved it.

"Call and fix an appointment to see her." Ade advised.

"I will." Sam said.

Much later in his room, Sam called the woman and she asked him to come to the bookshop the next day at about 11am.

On Monday morning, Sam got ready. At 10.30am, he left his room and walked to the bookshop with the hope that he would get the job. Eighteen minutes after, he reached the place. As he pushed the door open and stepped in, the bell above the door sounded. He approached a young lady at the counter and greeted her.

"I'm here to see Mrs. Payne." He said.

"Do you have an appointment to see her?" The lady asked.

"Yes." Sam answered.

"Okay. I will inform her right away." She said and got up.

While Sam waited, he looked around. He could see nine customers, picking different books. There were three shelves close to the entrance. Small gift items were displayed on one, greeting cards were on the second one while the third shelf featured new books. Bibles were in an area, and there were sections for books on religion, cooking, gardening, fiction and non-fiction. Children's books were in another area while CDs and tapes were toward the back of the large room.

The front door opened and the bell sounded. Sam looked in the direction and saw a couple.

"Hello." A female voice called out from behind Sam and he turned. The lady at the counter was back.

"You may go in. Her office is the last room on the right." She told him.

"Okay, thank you." Sam said and left in search of the room.

Soon, he was in front of the office. He knocked and entered, greeting Mrs. Payne.

"Please sit down." She told him.

The interview lasted about thirty minutes.

Mrs. Payne sat back and asked, "Can you start in a week's time?"

"Yes."

She looked at her table calendar and said, "Come on Tuesday, December 7, to start."

"It's okay. I'll be here."

She told Sam the bookshop opened to customers at 9am and closed at 8pm, but his working hours would be eight to five in the evening, Monday to Friday.

They talked about his salary and she agreed to pay him the same amount he got at Best Insurance Company. Sam was elated.

In the evening, he called Ann and told her he had found another job and would be resuming the following Tuesday.

****

After service on Sunday, Sam and another man came to Ann.

"Both of us have been asked to visit Pastor John whose wife has just put to bed."

Ann glanced at her watch. "Can I go with you?"

"I guess so." Sam said and looked at the second man.

"She can go with us. Maybe she doesn't want to leave you yet." The man said and laughed.

Sam smiled and looked at Ann.

She denied the man's statement immediately. "I just feel like going with you to see him. That's all."

As usual, Ann gave Sam the key to her car. Sam opened the doors and entered. The man opened the back door.

"No, you can sit in front." Ann told him.

"Are you sure?" He asked, laughing.

"What do you mean by that?" Sam asked him.

"I mean she should sit beside you."

"Oh, come off it." Ann said and laughed.

Later that evening, Sam sent a text message to Ann, to remind her to send text messages to the people she had invited for her birthday celebration.

On Tuesday, he got to Penny Books at 7.50am. At a little after eight, Mrs. Payne arrived.

"I'd like to show you around." She told him.

She introduced him to her six staff after which she took him on a tour of the whole office. She took him to a small room which she said would be his office. There was a computer on the table in the room.

By the time the tour was over, it was already 9am. The front door was opened and shortly after, customers began to come in. Sam stayed in the bookshop, watching and learning how work was being done.

The door opened again and Sam turned to see who had just come in. It was an elderly man. Sam went to him and greeted him. The man wanted Oral Robert's autobiography.

Sam went with him to look for it. They found it. The man took it and went to pay. The cashier rang up the sale, took a plastic bag from under the table and put the book in it.

"Thank you and have a nice day sir." Sam told the man as he turned to leave.

In the evening, he didn't leave at 5pm but waited thirty minutes more. When he eventually left, he went straight to class for lectures.

At about 9pm, Ann called his cell phone.

"So, how's the new place?"

Sam laughed and began to tell her about his first day at Penny Books.

 # Chapter 8

On Friday which was Ann's birthday, Sam sent a text message to her.

The day of the party dawned clear and bright. Sam arrived at about 7am with the four ladies who would cook and two men from the fellowship. He was in well-worn jeans and a blue shirt that was untucked, with the sleeves rolled up.

Smiling, Ann said, "Thanks for coming."

"No problem." They said. "We're glad we can help."

While the ladies were in the kitchen, Sam and the men were busy getting the party place ready. They arranged the chairs and tables that were brought in and set the canopy up.

Soon, Ann's mother and brother came.

At about 2pm, Mummie and eleven people from the fellowship arrived in the fellowship bus, to decorate the party place.

A banner on which was written 'Happy Birthday, Ann Lola Sankey' was hung by the high table where the celebrant and family would sit. Plates, cutleries, glass cups and napkins were neatly arranged on each table.

Balloons of two colors, white and yellow to match Ann's dress were used to decorate the place. A cluster of them was put by the table where the cake would be placed. These clusters were also hung at strategic places.

By 3.40pm, Ann was dressed and ready. She wore a beautiful yellow gown with sequins and matching accessories. Her hair was packed up beautifully with pins. With a well made up face, she looked sophisticated.

By 3.45pm, there were thirty two people from the church, nine from Ann's office and twenty of her friends including Pastor Emma. The rest of the people were relatives.

At 4.10pm, the celebration began with an opening prayer by Mummie. This was followed by praise and worship, led by Sylvester, and then choreography by Grace. Biodun handled the camera.

Sam moved around to make sure everyone was comfortable and everything went on well. He frequently came to Ann and talked in a low tone to get her approval on issues.

When Ann was asked to talk, she started by introducing her mother and brother, and thanked her parents for their love. She also introduced Mr. and Mrs. Noah and thanked them as well. She specially thanked Mr. Noah for encouraging her to return to the country, saying if she had not come back, she wouldn't have become a believer, and she wouldn't have had the peace and joy that were now hers.

The people clapped.

Next, she told them how she became a believer.

As Sam listened, he was impressed and grateful to God that he was a part of her story.

She ended it by singing the entire Amazing Grace hymn which she had memorized as a student in a Methodist High School.

The people clapped again.

Pastor John came up to give the word of exhortation which lasted about twenty minutes. Then he prayed for Ann and her family.

Ann cut her beautiful cake which was a gift from Mrs. Noah. Friends and family took pictures with her. When it was time for presentation of gifts, the choir leader stood beside her, taking the gifts from her.

Notebooks with Ann's picture on the cover were given to everyone present as gifts from Ann's mother.

By about 7pm, most of the guests had left. It remained ten people from the fellowship, including Sam and Mummie. They cleaned up the venue and returned the rented chairs and tables. When they were ready to leave at about 8.30pm, Ann gave them food to take away.

"I'll see you tomorrow." She told them as they entered the fellowship bus.

In the living room, her mother commented, "Those people did a good job. They are good friends."

Together with Mr. and Mrs. Noah, they began to discuss the party and all that happened. They were all clearly impressed.

Later in her room, she checked her phone and saw two missed calls from Daniel. She called him.

"I'm sorry I missed your party. How did it go?" He asked.

She told him about it.

"Was Sam there?"

"Of course, he was. He came with other fellowship members."

"Look, I think your friendship with him is going beyond ordinary."

She found the statement funny and laughed.

"I'm serious!" He said. "How can I be certain you're not sleeping with him while giving me some silly excuses?"

She stopped laughing. "Daniel, I feel highly insulted!"

"I didn't mean to insult you but … I mean, I don't understand what you're trying to do. I don't know what you're doing there while I'm here! I might have to look for someone else if there's no change from your end."

"Well, for your information, there's not going to be any change from my end, so you might as well go ahead and do whatever you want to do! I'm now a Christian!"

"And who told you I'm not a Christian?"

"Look Daniel, the truth is that we can't continue together. Things have changed. Let's end the relationship now!"

There she had said it! She listened for his response.

"I'll be back in Lagos towards the end of the year." He said.

He didn't talk about it! "Did you hear what I said?" She asked.

"I did but it's not something we can discuss on phone. When I get to Lagos, I'll see you."

"Fine. Look Daniel, I'm tired. I need to rest. Call me some other time, okay?"

"I'll call you tomorrow."

"Okay. And … go to church tomorrow." She mentioned two churches.

"Look, don't try to change me even if you have changed. I'll call you tomorrow."

"Okay. Goodnight." She said, yawning tiredly.

"Goodnight."

She tossed the phone on the bed and began to open her gifts. She got a yellow skirt suit from Agape Campus Church and a small purse from Mummie. A big box had Sam's name on it and she wondered what was inside as she opened it. It was a purple hat.

"Wow! This is beautiful!" She said to herself. It must have cost Sam some money.

Pastor Sam gave her a purse.

She sent a text message to Sam, the President and Mummie, to appreciate them.

When she had finished opening all the twenty three gifts, she knelt down beside her bed and thanked God for His blessings and grace upon her life.

Afterward, she removed the pins in her hair, had a shower and got in bed, where she relived the day.

The next day, she went for service. Afterward, she thanked them all for their support and gifts. When they were ready to leave, she told Ade, Mummie and Sam that she brought food and drinks for them.

"We can go to the hostel."

They entered her car, with Mummie sitting beside her in front and the men at the back.

Her phone began to ring. With her left hand on the wheel, she searched her purse for her phone, and picked the call. It was her father, to apologize for not making her birthday celebration.

In Mummie's room, they sat down and began to eat. Ann took her phone and sent a text message to Sam.

I have some pieces of fried meat in the car for you.

Sam's phone alerted him of a text message. He was talking so he said, "Excuse me."

He opened the message and read it. He smiled and continued talking without looking at Ann.

When Ann was ready, they saw her off to her car.

While the others were still talking, she opened the car and brought out a black plastic bag which she gave to Sam.

He took it and said, "Okay, thanks."

Some minutes after, she drove off.

On Sam's way to his room, he met Sylvester.

"How are you?" Sylvester asked.

"I'm fine."

"I've been to your room."

"Oh. I was in Mummie's room."

"Has Ann left?"

Sam nodded. "She has just left."

"Look Sam, I've been wanting to ask you. Are you going out with Ann?"

Sam smiled. "No. Why did you ask?"

"I've just been wondering. You are very close. And at her birthday party yesterday, your eyes seemed to follow her around. I sensed something."

So, he was being watched. He would have to be careful, Sam thought. Had Ann realized he had feelings for her?

He laughed.

"Tell me the truth." Sylvester prodded.

"That's the truth. We're just friends. There's nothing between us."

"Are you sure?"

Sam laughed again and nodded. "That's it."

"Is she in a relationship?"

Sam shrugged. "That's not really my business. You can ask her when you see her. Why did you go to my room?"

"That's what I wanted to ask you. If there's nothing between you, then you're getting too close."

"What do you mean? Am I the only one she's close to? She's close to the president as well. All of us were together in Mummie's room."

"Ade's friendship is different from yours. Ade has a fiancée."

Sam laughed. "I don't know what you're talking about. And don't forget, I brought her to the fellowship, which could be the reason she relates more with me."

"That's true." Sylvester agreed.

They talked some more and Sam went to his room.

In bed, Sam began to consider his feelings for Ann. He had been fighting them but could God be involved? Did she feel anything for him? What about Daniel? Was she still in a relationship with him? What about Pastor Emma?

She was growing in the faith and seemed to know what God wanted concerning certain things. She should be able to determine God's will in this situation as well. He began to pray, asking God to direct him.

What was she doing now?

He looked at the time, it was 7pm. He took his cell phone and called her.

"What are you doing?"

"I'm in the living room, watching TV."

They began to talk about her birthday.

"Did anyone come from your office?"

"Yes, nine people came."

"Wow!"

"They gave me good gifts. One of them, Odein gave me matching shoes and bag. In fact, the color matches the hat you gave me."

"That's nice."

Suddenly the line went off. There was no more air time on his phone. Just as he was putting the phone down, it began to ring. She had called him back and they concluded their conversation.

****

At about 7pm, Pastor Emma called Ann and told her he was on his way to her house.

"I'm at home."

When he arrived, Mrs. Noah got up and went into the bedroom.

As he sipped the juice Ann gave him, they talked. Ann thanked him for coming for her birthday and his gift.

Putting his glass cup down, he leaned forward and said, "Ann, I've come to really like you. I've been observing you and I think you possess the qualities I want in a woman. I want you to pray about me. I'd like to marry you."

Ann smiled. *A marriage proposal from a Christian? At last!*

Even though she was very happy as this was what she had been praying for, she didn't think she should give an answer yet. She needed to be very sure as she didn't know much about him.

"I'll pray about it and give you an answer as soon as possible." She promised.

"That's good enough for me."

"Let me ask you, how old are you?" She asked.

"I'm thirty three years old."

Hmm, he was nine years older than her. It wasn't too much.

"Why have you not gotten married?"

"The answer is simple. I've not met the right person."

"Have you ever been in a relationship?"

He sat back. "Well, yes."

"Please tell me about it."

"Er, we had a good relationship and we were planning to get married but she had some funny behaviors. There's something about me, I can tolerate a lot of things, but I can't tolerate dishonesty and unfaithfulness."

"Was she unfaithful to you?"

"She was a lot of things. No one is perfect though. I lost my temper with her once or twice and ... we had to call it quit eventually."

Hmm. Ann took a deep breath.

"As I said, I'll pray about it and give you my answer soon."

The next day, he came to her office and they went to the lunch hour fellowship together.

On Tuesday morning, Ann received a text message from Sam.

The chicken I planned sending to u today 4 Xmas escaped to a nearby church shouting - I shall not die but live to declare the glory of God. Pls, what do we do now since the chicken is now born again?

She laughed, and then sent a reply.

Let us leave the chicken alone.

In the evening, just before she left the office, Sam came and gave her a card and a yellow purse with sequins and beads, for Christmas.

"Oh Sam, you shouldn't have bothered to give me a purse. Didn't you see my text message? I told you to leave the chicken alone."

He smiled. "One of my friends sent that text message to me."

"You gave me a gift for my birthday just on Saturday."

"That was for your birthday. This is for Christmas." He pointed out.

"Thanks a lot."

Sam told her the University would be on Christmas break from December 22 to January 3, but because of his job, he would be on campus.

On Saturday, she made her Christmas shopping, bought cards and gifts for family and friends. She also bought a shirt and a pair of fine shoes for Sam, and a bag of rice for his family. She gave Pastor Emma a tie and a card.

On December 19, when Ann attended service at Agape Campus Church, she gave Sam the gifts. He was both surprised and impressed.

They talked and he said he would visit her at home on December 26.

On Christmas day, he called to wish her a merry Christmas.

****

On the last day of the year, Ann closed early from work. As she was getting ready to sleep at about 5pm, so she would wake up at 9pm and go for Watch-night service at the church in her neighborhood, she received a text message from Sam.

Welcome on board to Dec airways, flight 031 days and we'll be flying @ 100% success level and 30000 ft above failure. Tighten ur seatbelt and relax as we are about to take off with pilot Jesus en route Collaboration of Mercies and Grace Airport. We shall stop over @ Divine Breakthrough, Massive Prosperity, and Abundant Blessings Airports. You and your family will surely land safely @ Collaboration of Mercies and Grace Airport. Have a safe flight.

Reading it twice, she planned to send a reply when she woke up but forgot. She was already in service before she remembered. Immediately after the Watch-night service at 1am, she sent a message to him.

B4 d network gets busy, b4 d texts get too many, b4 d calls get chaotic, b4 d new yr celebration ends, let me be among d first to say have a fruitful & exciting new year ahead.

****

On the 7th of January which was Friday, Daniel returned to Lagos. He called Ann in the evening.

"I'm back but I'll be going to one of my friends' house tomorrow. I will spend up to four days there."

"Why are you going there?"

"Nothing. I promised him some time ago that I would come and spend some time with him. He's my very good friend."

"Okay."

"Can you come there tomorrow? We need to see to talk."

Ann did a quick thinking. She should see him and terminate the relationship.

"Okay. I'll go to my parents' house first. Tomorrow is my dad's birthday. On my way back, I'll stop to see you."

"That's fine."

He gave her the address. It was in an Estate.

"I'll be expecting you." He said.

On Saturday morning, Ann put the clothes, shoes, and jewelries she would wear at her parents' place in an overnight bag, and left with her uncle's family at about 8.30am.

Shortly after, Sam phoned her.

"When are you leaving for your parents' house?"

"We are on the way already."

We? "Who are you going with? Your uncle's family?"

"Yes. I'm in their car." She said.

"Oh, okay. My regards to them."

"Alright."

"When will you be back at home?" He asked.

"Er ... I don't know, maybe by six. Daniel is around and -"

"Daniel? When did he come?"

"Yesterday. When I leave my parents' house, I'll go to his place. I need to sort out the issue of our relationship once and for all."

"Okay. I'll call you later. Bye." Sam said.

Ann returned the cell phone into her purse.

They reached her parents' house at a little after 10am.

Ann changed her clothes and dressed up for the ceremony. By 11am, most of the people the family was expecting had come and the birthday ceremony began with a short prayer from one of Mr. Sankey's friends.

While they were all eating at about 12.30pm, Mr. Noah received a call. Then he got up and announced he had to leave for an urgent meeting.

"Ann, I'm sorry I won't be able to take you back home." He said.

"That's alright. I've just remembered that I'm supposed to check Daniel."

"Is he around?" He asked.

"Yes. I think he returned yesterday. I will be going to see him."

"Alright. We'll meet at home."

"Yes, Uncle."

At about 3pm, when Ann was ready to leave her parents' house, she changed from the lace *iro* and *buba* she wore, to a pink blouse, and black slacks. After saying goodbye to her parents and the few relatives who remained, she left, carrying her overnight bag.

She got a cab that took her to the Estate where she was to meet Daniel. She got down in front of the house at about 4pm and saw Daniel's SUV in the compound. *He's here, good.*

She went to the second floor by the spiral stairs. When she pressed the bell, the door was opened by a big, fair lady.

"You must be Ann." The lady said brightly. "Please come in.

Daniel appeared behind her. "Oh, you're here."

Ann entered. A stocky man came out of a room.

Daniel introduced them. "Ann, meet Dare and Nina."

"We're happy to meet you." Dare told her. "Daniel has told us so much about you. Please sit down and make yourself comfortable."

Ann sat and glanced around. The walls were adorned with photographs of Dare and Nina. They must be married, she thought.

Daniel brought two bottles of soft drinks and two glass cups. Placing them on a side table in front of Ann, he sat beside her. He opened the drinks and poured them in the glass cups.

"Thanks." She told him.

He took her left hand. "I've missed you, you know."

She pulled her hand away from his. "You know I told you something on phone."

"Yes, you did. We need to talk. That was why I asked you to come over."

She used her right hand to carry her glass cup and took a sip. Then she said, "I can't be in a relationship with you again, Daniel. I'm sorry but we are no longer compatible."

"Are you sure you have thought of this carefully?"

She nodded slowly. "I have. For our benefit, it has to end."

Daniel stared at her.

She went on. "I'm sorry if this will hurt you in any way but ... believe me, this is the right thing for us to do."

Nina came over. "Please Ann, when you finish your drink, I'd like you to assist me in the kitchen."

"Okay. I'll soon be with you." Ann replied.

Nina returned to the kitchen.

Ann turned back to Daniel. "I'm sorry if -"

Dare chose that time to talk. "So, Daniel, when are you guys getting married?"

Daniel laughed. "Well, like you, I'm not ready to be chained down yet. Marriage chains you to one spot."

The two men laughed.

Ann turned to look at Daniel. *So, Dare and Nina are not married.*

"I was only joking." Daniel said, raising a hand in surrender.

"That's okay. You're entitled to your opinion." Ann said. Their relationship was over as far as she was concerned. His statement did not matter to him.

"Does Nina live with him?" She asked Daniel in a whisper.

He nodded.

Dare asked Daniel a question.

Ann quickly finishing her drink, put her purse on the seat beside Daniel and made to get up.

"Why don't you remove your shoes, so you can be comfortable?" Daniel suggested.

She did and put them beside her overnight bag, which was on a side.

Her phone began to ring. She opened her purse and brought it out. It was her uncle.

"Hello, Uncle, good afternoon - yes - no - no, I'm with Daniel - okay, okay - thank you. Bye."

She pressed the end button and told Daniel, "That was my uncle. He sends his greetings."

She returned the phone into her purse and got up. She could see the kitchen where Nina was as the door was left open. She went there.

Nina was about to slice a plantain.

"Can you help me with these plantains? You'll slice and fry them."

"Okay." Ann drew close.

Nina carried a bowl and went out of the kitchen, closing the door.

Ann took a knife. When the door opened, she looked back and saw Daniel.

He came to her and held her by the waist. "Ann,"

"No!" She said firmly and wriggled out of his arms.

"Relax."

"No!" She repeated.

He grinned. "What are you doing?"

"I want to slice and fry these plantains."

"Okay, when you finish, let's continue with our discussion."

"Okay."

He went out of the kitchen.

Nina returned, brought dishes out of the cabinet and left again.

When Ann finished frying the plantains, she carried the bowl and opened the door. Nina was setting the table.

"It's ready." Ann told her and set the bowl on the table.

"Look, I'm hungry." Dare said, coming over to the table. "Is food ready?"

"Yes." Nina answered.

"Daniel, come over." Dare called out.

Ann was walking back to her seat when Daniel caught her hand.

"Let's join them at the table."

"No. I'm not hungry. I ate at my parents' place."

"No. You have to eat something, even if only a little." Dare said.

"You have to eat." Nina added. "Even if it's plantain. Nobody comes here without eating."

Ann decided to join them at the table.

Nina served her food and Dare's. Daniel served himself. Ann didn't make any move.

"Eat something, Ann." Daniel said.

She took a small plate and put some slices of plantain. They got ready to eat.

"Can we pray?" Ann asked, and looked at Daniel for approval.

He didn't seem too happy at the suggestion.

Dare and Nina smiled.

"Alright. That's fine." Dare said.

Ann prayed briefly and they said 'Amen'.

As they began to eat, Nina asked, "Which church do you attend?"

Ann told her.

Daniel spoke, "It was when she returned from S.A that she met this guy who has been influencing her. It's always been about God, since then. As a matter of fact, she's here to terminate our relationship. Can both of you please talk to her? I mean, what she's doing doesn't make sense. She's becoming too stubborn for my liking."

Dare drank a little water. As he put the glass cup down he said, "Ann, it's not a bad thing to go to church. There are times we also go to a church but becoming a fanatic is wrong. A person should strike a balance."

"That is it!" Nina said in agreement with Dare.

Dare went on, "You're too beautiful for that religious nonsense. You'd better not allow yourself to be misled."

"Yes, you should be careful, Ann. All that church stuff is rubbish." Nina added.

Daniel spoke again. "I really like Ann but she's allowing this religious stuff get between us."

Dare spoke again. "That's the problem! You'd better not allow it to affect your relationship with Daniel."

Nina added, "You should be grateful to have a man like Daniel who is tall and handsome. Do you know how many girls would love to have him?"

Daniel continued eating.

Ann didn't respond.

Nina went on. "He's well educated and from a well-to-do family."

Ann sighed.

Daniel dropped his cutleries, "We may leave all that aside. But Ann, the fact that I'm coming after you should mean something. You're not being fair to me."

Ann finally spoke, "Daniel, could we talk about this later?"

"These guys are my friends and they know everything that's happening."

Ann shook her head sadly. They couldn't be her friends as they obviously did not love her God.

Nina spoke again. "Why did you shake your head? You think we are sinners, right?" She laughed cynically. "You guys are deceiving yourselves."

"I'm sorry to say but some of you guys are very parochial, very narrow minded." Dare said angrily.

Ann didn't talk, realizing she could not win the argument. They outnumbered her and were not ready to listen.

They eventually finished eating.

"Help me bring the dishes to the kitchen please." Nina told Ann, as she walked to the kitchen with glass cups.

Ann did and assisted her in the kitchen to clean up.

She returned to the living room and sat. Daniel came to sit beside her.

"So, how do we get to talk? I'll need to leave soon." She told Daniel.

"Do you realize you've not been fair to me?"

Ann frowned. "How?"

Just then, the doorbell rang. Nina went to get it, and a man and a lady entered. Daniel seemed to know them as well as he greeted the couple familiarly.

As the couple was talking with Dare and Nina, Ann tapped Daniel's hand.

"Yes?"

"I have to leave. It's getting late." She said.

"Okay. We'll talk outside."

She looked for her purse but couldn't find it. "Where's my purse?"

He got up for her to check where he sat but it wasn't there either.

"Are you looking for something?" Dare asked.

"Yes." Ann said.

"She's looking for her purse." Daniel supplied.

"Where is it?" Nina asked.

"Where did you put it?" Dare asked.

"It was here." Ann pointed at the seat.

"I'm sure you'll soon find it." Nina said and excused herself, going inside the bedroom.

Ann frowned in confusion. "I left it here when I was going to the kitchen. My cell phone and money are inside it."

She walked over to her bag, opened it and checked but it wasn't there. Then she noticed that her shoes were not where she put them.

She smiled. Someone must have taken them. It must be some kind of joke. She went back to sit.

"Have you seen it?" Daniel asked.

Shaking her head, she told him quietly, "Even my shoes are gone. Daniel, did you take them?"

He smiled innocently, "Take them? Why should I?"

"Okay. Can you ask your friends please? It's getting late. I have to go. Tomorrow is Sunday."

Dare and the couple were talking.

"I'll ask Nina." He said and got up. Walking to a door, he knocked and entered. He emerged about a minute after and returned to Ann's side.

Talking in a whisper, he said, "Nina doesn't know anything about it. Let's wait until the visitors leave."

Ann asked, also in a whisper, "Until they leave? When will that be?"

"Soon, I hope."

She took a deep breath, glanced at her watch and sat back.

As the visitors were leaving at about 7pm, Nina came out and together with Dare, saw them off.

As soon as the door closed behind them, Ann asked Daniel, "How will I get home?"

"I'll get a cab for you."

"So, who among you took my things?"

"I'm serious. I don't know anything about it."

"When your friends return, get my things for me, please."

"Okay."

Ann spoke again. "So, what do you mean by I've not been fair to you?"

They continued talking.

About ten minutes after, Dare and Nina were not back. Now Ann was getting angry.

Checking her watch again, she exclaimed, "What? 7.15pm!" She looked at Daniel. "Now, what's going on? What's this all about?"

"I really don't know but you'll be fine. You're with me. Relax."

"How can I relax? Look at the time! They'll be expecting me at home!"

"Your uncle knows you're with me. You can sleep here if it comes to that. You're a big girl, come on!"

She glared at him. "I'm a big girl but I don't do that!"

"Hey, you're with me!" He laughed.

"And if I'm going to sleep outside, shouldn't that be my decision? Why should my things be taken?"

"I haven't said your things were taken so you could spend the night here!"

She hissed impatiently. "Can you please go outside and call them? I need to leave now!"

"Alright."

Sighing, he got up, wore his slippers and went out. Ann began to pray quietly, asking God for help.

It took about five minutes before he came back. "They are coming." He said.

Another five minutes, Dare and Nina entered, talking and laughing.

Ann stood up, ready to get her things and leave. Daniel remained seated.

"Oka-a-a-y, Ann and Daniel," Dare began as he sat down.

Nina sat beside him and said, "Look Ann, I took your things, so calm down."

Ann was surprised at what Nina had just said and the way she said it. What was the game? How could she tell her to calm down?

She sat down, shaking her legs. "Okay, I'm all ears. What is it, Nina?"

"Nothing." Nina raised her hands. "I want you to sleep here."

"Wha-t? You want me to sleep here?" Ann asked.

"Yes." Nina said without hesitation. "You'll spend the night here with Daniel. So, relax."

"Shouldn't that be my business? Shouldn't it be my decision?" Ann asked.

"We are making the decision for you."

"That's very funny." Ann laughed in disbelief.

Nina also laughed.

"Now, if this is some kind of joke, stop it!" Ann glared at her.

"Ann, please." Daniel said.

"*Ann, please*, what?!" Ann shouted. "Is this what you planned?"

Daniel shook his head. "I told you I didn't know anything about it. I'm as surprised as you are but really, I'll want you to spend the night with me."

"Daniel, you know that's not possible! I'm a Christian!"

"Oh, please!" Nina said with a grimace. She stood up and entered the bedroom.

Ann looked at Dare. "Please, I need to leave. I have to get home. Could you please talk to her?"

"I already have but it appears she has made up her mind. You can leave very early tomorrow morning, I can drive you to your house."

"It has to be tonight. Can you get me a cab or drive me down, please?" Ann pleaded with Dare.

"I don't plan to go out this night, I'm sorry. I'll take you home tomorrow morning."

"That's not possible!" Ann shook her head.

"Oh, well."

"Don't you understand?" She turned and looked at Daniel for help. "Daniel, please!"

"Ann, come on! Spend the night here. Enjoy yourself."

She took a deep breath, trying to think of what to do next.

"Excuse me." Dare stood up and walked toward the bedroom.

Ann stood angrily. "Please call Nina!" She told Dare. "I have to get my things and leave, now or I'll scream this place down!"

Daniel stood up too. "Ann, don't embarrass yourself, alright? These people are my friends."

"I mean it! If I don't get my things now, I'll scream this place down!" She repeated.

"Okay, go ahead!" Daniel said.

Dare continued toward the room.

"GIVE ME MY THINGS NOW!!!" Ann shouted.

Dare looked back briefly, then proceeded to the room and entered, closing the door.

Ann almost couldn't believe what was happening. "This must be a dream!"

Then she looked at Daniel. "I thought you once said you cared about me."

"I still do but -"

"How can you care about me and do this to me? That's not caring, that's wickedness!" She told him. "I know you have a hand in this."

"I don't."

"Alright. Take me home. You can bring my purse and shoes whenever you like."

"You will find this difficult to believe but my car didn't start when I wanted to go out this afternoon."

"DANIEL!" Ann shouted.

He threw the car key to her. "Go and check it yourself. Why would I lie?"

"Daniel, don't do this to me! Don't let me hate you!"

"My car doesn't start, I'm serious!"

Ann glared at him, "What will happen? Can I get a cab?"

"This is an estate. You can't get a cab unless you get to the gate. I'll suggest you change your plans and leave tomorrow morning. I'm in that room." He pointed at a door.

"You can take the bed while I sleep on the floor." He pulled her hand.

She jerked away. "Don't touch me!"

"Ann, look,"

"How could you do this to me?"

"Do what? What have I done wrong?" He stared at her. "I didn't plan this with Dare and his girlfriend, you have to believe me."

"If you didn't plan it, then get my things from them and let me leave."

"You don't know Nina. Once she's determined to do something, she won't change."

Ann remained quiet.

"Okay, I'm sorry, Ann." He was looking at her.

"Can I use your phone?"

"Okay." He checked where he was sitting. "I can't find my phone too. She must have taken it."

"That's good, and you want me to believe you and your friends didn't plan this?"

"I didn't plan it with them. She took my phone as well. Do you want something to drink?"

She ignored his question and asked, "Where are your friends?"

"They must have gone in to sleep."

She kept quiet.

"Give me a minute please." He said and entered the second room, closing the door.

Ann looked round the living room. She hoped she was safe. If something should happen to her, there was no way she could call anyone on phone.

The door opened and Daniel returned. "I'll suggest you come and lie down. You will leave in the morning."

She didn't move. She didn't trust him and she was determined she would not close her eyes.

She sat down. Daniel did the same. There was silence for a couple of minutes.

"What could make you change your mind?" Daniel asked.

Ann didn't respond as she thought of what she could do to leave the house. She couldn't walk to the gate, it was far. Besides, she had her overnight bag to carry.

After some minutes, Daniel spoke again, "I need to sleep. Are you coming?"

"No."

"Goodnight." He got up.

"Daniel!" She called him.

He stopped.

"You shocked me this evening."

He sighed.

"And if these people are your friends, then you are dangerous."

"Hey, stop! They meant well. I'm sure they did what they did with the hope that you would stay and we would resolve our issue."

She shook her head.

Daniel went back to the room and closed the door.

Ann remained where she was, shaking her legs as she prayed. Soon, she became tired. After about five minutes, she became sleepy and soon, slept off.

She suddenly woke up when she heard her name. It was Daniel calling her. He was in pyjamas.

"Come and sleep on the bed so you can be comfortable."

"No."

"I promise not to touch you."

"No."

He returned to the room.

She started praying again to keep awake but soon slept.

She woke up at 6.45am. Oh my God! Quickly getting up, she walked to the room Daniel was in and knocked the door.

He came out, stretching.

"It's 6.45am. I have to leave now. Get my purse and shoes please."

He used a hand to clear his face and looked at the wall clock. "Alright. I'll be with you soon."

He returned to the room. When he emerged about a minute later, he was dressed up.

"Where's the toilet?" She asked.

He pointed at a door and she went there. When she came out, she asked for her purse and shoes again.

"They are there."

She looked and saw them on top of her bag. "This is unbelievable."

"They meant well, Ann. And I was desperate enough to do anything. I'm sorry."

"What you did was wrong!" She stared at him. "You and your friends forced me to spend the night here?" She shook her head.

"Well, I'm sorry."

She brought her cell phone out and checked. She had eighteen missed calls, nine of them from Sam, four from her uncle and five from Pastor Emma. There were also six text messages. She returned the phone into her purse.

They left the house with Daniel carrying her overnight bag. They walked to the gate where she got a cab.

"I'll call you." Daniel said.

She didn't respond as the car moved.

Her phone began to ring. She took it and checked. It was Mr. Noah and she picked it.

She told him, "Something happened. I'm on my way now. I'll explain to you - what did you say? - yes, I'm okay. Bye."

 **Chapter 9**

As she was returning the phone into her purse, it began to ring again. This time it was Sam.

Tiredly, she picked it. "Hello?"

"Ann? Is that Ann?"

"Yes."

"I've been calling you since yesterday evening. Where are you?"

"I'm on my way home. I'll call you later."

"Are you alright?" He sounded concerned.

"I am."

"Okay. I'll see you in church."

"Okay."

Before he could say anything further, she ended the call and sighed. She was feeling sleepy but she refused to give in to sleep as she had heard of bad things that happened to people in cabs. She had just come out of one ordeal, she didn't want to get into another.

She began to read the text messages to keep awake. Two were from Sam, three from Pastor Emma and one from Biodun.

Soon, she got home and went inside. Mr. and Mrs. Noah were in the living room. She sat down tiredly, dropping her bag.

"What happened? Where are you coming from?" They asked with concern.

Taking a deep breath, she said, "It was Daniel."

"What about him?"

She didn't know how to start and suddenly, she found tears gathering in her eyes, and they began to spill over.

Mr. and Mrs. Noah were surprised.

Mrs. Noah quickly got up and came to sit beside her. "What is it? What happened to you?"

"It was Daniel. I told you I was going to see him."

They nodded.

She told them how her things were taken and she couldn't leave.

Husband and wife looked at each other.

"That was rubbish!" Mr. Noah said angrily. "How could they have done that?"

"Are you okay though?" Mrs. Noah asked.

She nodded, wiping her face with the back of her hand.

"That's the most important thing. Do you want me to call him or get him arrested by the police?" Mr. Noah wanted to know.

She shook her head. "It may not be necessary."

"What if he repeats such a thing?"

She shook her head. "I've ended the relationship."

"Good."

"I need to go and rest."

"Okay."

Ann got up, took her bag and went into her room.

Mr. Noah nudged his wife and nodded in the direction of Ann. "Follow her. Try to find out if any other thing happened to her so we would know what to do."

"Alright." She said and followed Ann.

In the room, Ann was about to enter the bathroom when she heard a knock on the door.

"Ann?"

"Yes, Aunty? I'm coming."

She opened the door and stepped back to allow Mrs. Noah enter.

"Are you sure there's nothing else you need to tell us?" Mrs. Noah asked.

Ann shook her head.

"Did he rape you or something?"

"No, nothing like that happened." Ann said.

When she assured Mrs. Noah that she was alright and there was nothing else to say, Mrs. Noah left.

Ann entered the bathroom. When she came out, she decided she would have to sleep. She couldn't go for service. Realizing some people might try to reach her, she turned off her phone. She didn't want to see or talk to anyone right now. She got on the bed and slept.

****

Throughout the service, Sam kept expecting Ann to enter but she did not. He felt concerned. Where was she last night that she didn't pick his several calls and did not call him back? She hadn't replied his text messages either.

When she eventually picked his call this morning, she hadn't sounded too good. And now, she wasn't in church. What could the problem be? She had said she would visit Daniel. Could it have something to do with him?

Immediately the service ended, he took his phone and dialed her cell phone again. It was switched off. He frowned. This was the first time her phone would be switched off. Something was definitely wrong. He tried to guess what it might be but wasn't sure.

Some people came to ask him about her and he simply told them she couldn't come.

At 2pm, he called her line again, it was still switched off. He went to his room but remained restless and disturbed. Deciding to switch the TV on, he used the remote control to search the channels for an interesting program or movie.

He found a movie being shown on one and he increased the volume. It was about a young girl whose poor father needed medical attention. Being the first of seven children, the teenage girl determined to raise the money her father would need for surgery. She met a man who seemed sympathetic and promised to give her the money. He asked her to come to his house to collect the money and the girl did. As he locked the door and smiled, looking at the girl, Sam had a feeling the man was going to do something bad to the girl. Remembering how Ann had almost been raped, Sam felt upset. Why do some men rape? He wondered, shaking his head.

Taking the control, he changed the channel. He didn't want a movie that would upset him further.

About an hour later, he tried Ann's line again. This time, it rang and she eventually picked it.

"Hello."

He felt she sounded dull. Had she just woken up and was feeling he was disturbing her?

"Hello, Ann." He said nicely. "How are you?"

"I'm fine."

"I thought you would come to church."

"I wanted to but I realized I needed to rest."

"That's fine. I hope I didn't wake you up."

"Not really."

"Is everything okay?"

"Yes."

There was a brief silence before he spoke again. "I have a feeling something happened to you yesterday."

"Er … well … yes but we can talk about it later."

"I sensed it and prayed for you." He said.

"Thank you."

"Er … I'd like to come and see you. Can I… come?"
She didn't reply immediately.

"Or … are you going to be busy?" He quickly said.

"No, no. You can come if you want. I'm not going out."

"Okay. What about your uncle?"

"It's okay."

"Alright. I'll be there shortly. Bye."

"Bye."

She got up and went to the bathroom to wash her face. Then she changed into a nice dress.

At about 4.30pm, Olu knocked on her door to announce the presence of Sam.

In the living room, Ann asked Sam, "Do you want something to drink?"

"No."

"Why?"

"I don't want anything. Er … can we sit outside or go somewhere nearby? I don't feel comfortable sitting in your uncle's house like this."

She smiled. "Let's go to the balcony."

At the balcony, they sat down.

"So, what happened to you?" His eyes searched hers.

She made a face. "Ugh, well, … I left my parents' house -" she stopped and smiled in a sad way. "If the whole thing wasn't so silly, I'd say it was funny."

He waited for her to continue.

She did. "Well, as I told you yesterday morning, Daniel called and said he'd want us to talk."

Daniel? Sam frowned. This might be worse than he thought.

"He said he was at a friend's place and I went there. When I was ready to leave, I discovered that my shoes and purse had been taken."

"Taken?"

She shrugged. "Yes. Apparently, he and his friends didn't want me to leave."

Sam was surprised at what he was hearing.

"Of course, they don't approve of my faith, they said a lot of things." She paused. "I ended up spending the night sitting down in the living room. That was it."

"So, you left this morning?"

"Yes."

He felt some parts of the story had not been said. So, he asked, "You were talking about his friends, how many of them?"

"Oh, it was just his friend, Dare and his girlfriend."

"I don't understand, why did they take your things, I mean, why should they?" Sam asked with a frown.

"They probably hoped I would change my mind concerning Daniel."

"What's the position of things between both of you now?"

"It's over, definitely."

"To spend the night … with Daniel?" He said, obviously finding the whole thing ridiculous. "But …was there no way you could have called me or someone for help?"

"My phone was in the purse that was taken, and they didn't give me theirs."

"Daniel did not give you his phone?"

She shook her head.

"How could they have done that?"

She didn't talk.

"But, are you okay?"

"I am."

Soon he left.

Some minutes after Ann returned to her room, Olu came again to tell her that Pastor Emma was around.

Tiredly, she went back to the living room to see him. One look at him where he sat told her he was very angry.

"So, where have you been, Ann? Where did you go?"

She didn't expect this anger from him. "I went somewhere."

"I know you went somewhere. What I want to know is where? Why didn't you pick my calls?"

Releasing an exasperated sigh, she said, "I'm sorry. The phone wasn't with me."

"Where was your phone? Where did you sleep?"

How did he know? She wondered.

"When you didn't pick my call and there was no reply to my text messages, I came here and your uncle didn't seem to know where you were as well."

So, he was here. Mr. and Mrs. Noah must have forgotten to tell me.

"I'm sorry."

"Where did you sleep?"

She didn't want to lie but something told her he would not understand if she mentioned Daniel.

So she sighed. "Look, I've already told you that -"

"Don't say you went somewhere!"

She smiled and got up to take the remote control of the TV.

He suddenly shot up from his seat and pulled her back roughly, she almost fell.

"You don't walk out on me when I'm talking to you!"

She was shocked. "I wasn't walking out on you. I wanted to take the remote."

"Remote for what?"

Still shocked, she smiled.

"I can slap you for that! Why are you smiling?"

She sat down. "You will slap me, Emma?"

"Yes, if you provoke me, I will!"

"Alright." She kept quiet.

He sat down. "I still want to know where you slept. I told you from the beginning that I want honesty. I hate lies or any form of deceit or unfaithfulness."

"I haven't been unfaithful to you because I'm not in a relationship with you yet. I haven't said I would marry you and you're treating me this way! You pushed me and I almost fell, you threatened to slap me!"

"Because you're not telling me the truth!"

"What truth, Emma? I've already said I went somewhere -"

"You didn't sleep at home!" He said.

"Does that mean I spent the night in a man's arms?"

He calmed down a little and they continued talking.

He eventually apologized. "I'm sorry. I'm not usually like this. I apologize."

"I'm surprised at the side of you I've just seen."

He smiled. "Don't worry. It won't happen again."

Some minutes after, he left.

On Monday, Pastor Emma came to her office at noon. He apologized again and promised to be careful not to lose his temper with her again.

She shrugged.

"Will you be going for fellowship?"

"No. I'll be going out soon for a meeting with one of my colleagues."

"Alright. I'll call you later."

At about 1.25pm, Ann and Odein left for the meeting. Odein talked non-stop till they reached where they were going. The same thing happened on their way back to the office. He told Ann he was a Christian. When he asked if she was a Christian and she said she was, he began to talk and complain about some people in his church.

When they finally reached the office and Ann was able to escape from him, she heaved a sigh of relief.

****

Fourth Saturday of January, Sam called Ann in the afternoon to say hello.

Giggling, she told him, "Hold on. Someone wants to talk to you."

"Hold it, Ann! Who is the person?" He quickly asked.

She laughed, "Hold on."

Sam frowned. He hoped the person was not her uncle.

"My VP!" A male voice said cheerfully.

Sam's frown deepened. That should be someone from his Agape Campus Church.

"Who is this?" He asked sharply.

The person laughed and said, "It's me, Sylvester."

Sam was shocked. "Sylvester? What are you doing in Ann's house?"

"What do you mean? I came to visit her."

Both surprised and angry at the answer, Sam asked, "You came to visit her … without telling me?"

"What do you mean?" Sylvester asked again. "Do I have to take permission from you before I can see her?"

Oh my God! Sam muttered under his breath. How could he be saying that in Ann's presence?

"Okay, forget it! We'll talk later. Could you please give back the phone to her?" Sam said.

Sylvester did.

"We'll talk later since you have a visitor now." Sam said angrily.

He expected Ann to say she hadn't invited him but she simply said okay.

That angered him further. He threw the phone on the bed and held his head with both hands. *What's going on, God? I didn't ask to fall in love with her. What do I do?*

He might have to let Ann know he loved her but as an executive member of Agape Campus Church, he must inform the president first.

Suddenly lifting his head, he took his phone. Scrolling down the contacts, he got the president's name and dialed.

"Are you in your room?" Sam asked.

"Yes. What's up?" Ade asked.

"I'm coming over to discuss an issue with you."

"Okay. I'll expect you."

Seven minutes after, he was sitting with the President in his room.

Ade noticed Sam's countenance. "You look upset. Is everything okay?"

"I guess so. I just want to inform you of a situation."

Ade sat up. "Go ahead. I'm all ears."

"I called Ann some minutes ago. Then she asked me to hold on to talk to someone. When the person came on, it was Sylvester."

"Sylvester?"

"Yes, Sylvester, in Ann's house." Sam paused and went on. "Of course, I was surprised and expressed it. Right there, in the presence of Ann, he asked me if he needed to take permission from me before visiting her!"

Ade took a deep breath.

Sam went on. "I knew Ann first. I brought her to the fellowship. She's not a student, she came through me. If he wanted to visit her, shouldn't he have told me? And as an executive member, if he's interested in a lady, shouldn't he inform the fellowship based on our rules?"

Ade nodded.

"Or has he told you he's interested in Ann?" Sam asked, half afraid of what Ade's answer would be.

Ade shook his head. "No, but let me ask you, are you in love with Ann?"

Sam took a deep breath. "I didn't plan it and I don't know how it happened but … yes, I am."

"I knew it." Ade said and began to laugh.

Smiling, Sam raised a hand to stop him. "I need to explain. I just invited her to church and that was all. There was nothing on my mind. But later on, I began to have feelings that there was something special about her. I felt God telling me that she is my wife. I was fighting the feelings, as I wasn't thinking of any relationship but the more I fought it, the more the feelings grew."

"Have you told her?"

Sam shook his head. "No."

"But there was a time I asked you about her, you said there was nothing."

"Yes, it was because I wasn't sure yet."

"But now you are?"

"I know how God talks to me and I know He's talking to me about her. I also know that I love her." Sam said.

"Wow!" Ade laughed. "That's serious."

Sam smiled.

"We will come back to the issue of Sylvester but I want us to discuss your feelings for her first. Do you think she feels the same way about you?"

"I don't know, and that's the truth."

"Do you know if she has someone?"

"Er, I don't think so." Then he remembered Ann mentioned Pastor Emma. So, he said, "Let me say I don't know."

Ade took a breath. "Okay, let's go back to Sylvester. He should have told one of us he was going to visit Ann, as he is an executive member."

He took his cell phone and pressed some buttons. Then he held the phone to his ear.

"Hello, how are you? - are you in your room? oh, okay, please see me in my room when you return. Bye."

Then he told Sam, "He's not back. When he returns, I will call you so we can discuss the issue together."

"Okay. Thanks."

Sam returned to his room. He took a book to read but couldn't concentrate.

What did he like about Ann? He asked himself. She was good and godly, she had passion for the things of God, she was quick to smile and laugh, she was beautiful, she asked for his opinion about issues and trusted his judgement ... He just liked everything about her, he realized.

He asked himself another question, was he ready to spend the rest of his life with her? His answer was yes. The more he thought of her, the surer he became.

At about 5.30pm, Ade called him.

"Can you come now? Sylvester is back."

"Alright."

Some minutes after, Sam was back in Ade's room.

Sylvester was seated. Sam greeted him but he answered a little coldly.

Ade told Sylvester the reason he asked him to come.

He went on. "I may have to agree with Sam. You should have told one of us that you were going to Ann's house. Firstly, she's not a student. Secondly, she worships with us because of the person she knows and that person is Sam. And if I may add, you have to be careful about visiting the opposite sex, more so because you're an executive member of the fellowship."

Ade then informed Sylvester of Sam's interest in Ann.

Sylvester looked at Sam angrily. "But I asked you if you were in a relationship with her!"

"Yes, you did and I said I wasn't. And still I'm not because I haven't told her anything." Sam explained.

"Sylvester, if I may ask, can you say that God has spoken to you concerning Ann?"

He shook his head. "I just wanted to get to know her better."

They continued talking and at the end, the issue was resolved, and Sylvester and Sam left together, friends again.

In his room, Sam began to pray. Lord, I don't know how to handle this. Am I wasting my time with Ann?

After service the next day, Ann waited as usual. Sam told her they would be going to Mummie's room as it was her birthday.

"Oh, really? Why didn't you tell me yesterday so I could get a gift for her?"

"I only got to know last night."

Ann noticed he wasn't his cheerful self, he seemed a bit withdrawn.

"Is everything alright?"

"What do you mean?" He asked sharply. How could she stand there and ask him that question? Didn't she realize she should have told him that Sylvester would be coming to visit her?

"You look a little upset."

"I'm fine. I need to go back to the others."

"Alright. I'll be by my car."

When Sam, Mummie and the president were ready, they came to meet Ann where she was standing by her car.

Ann congratulated Mummie, and promised her a gift.

"Are you going with us to my room?' Mummie asked her.

"Yes." She answered, opening her car doors.

Sam did not ask to drive but sat at the back. Mummie sat beside Ann in front while Ade sat beside Sam.

Soon they were in Mummie's room. About sixteen other people joined them. Sam made sure he did not sit beside Ann.

When Ann was ready to leave, she signaled at him. He got up and came to her.

"I have to leave."

"Okay. I'm ready when you are."

She took her purse and stood up.

Sam told the others they were leaving. Ann did the same and together, they left.

As they descended the staircase, Ann said, "You seem very quiet and withdrawn today. Is everything okay?"

"Yes. It's just that I have a lot on my mind."

Outside, they stood by her car.

"Aren't you going to ask me about Sylvester's visit?" Ann asked, smiling.

"I didn't want to push you. I knew you would tell me if you wanted to. I'm only surprised you didn't tell me he was coming to your place."

"Well, there wasn't much to it. I thought he was joking when he told me he would come. I was surprised to see him."

"What did he say?" Sam asked. That was the part that interested him.

"Nothing much. He said it was a courtesy call, although he was asking me some funny questions but … you know the way he is sometimes." She shrugged.

"What funny questions?"

"First, he wanted to know if I was in a relationship," she flipped her right hand, "… that sort of thing. And then, he asked about you."

Sam looked at her. "Asked you about me? What did he want to know?"

"He wanted to know if I was going out with you. Wasn't that funny?"

The look on her face said she found the idea ridiculous.

Sam did not respond immediately, as he thought of what to say. Then he asked, "And what did you say?"

"I told him that we're just friends."

When Sam didn't talk, she continued. "But it appeared he found it a little hard to believe. In the night, when I was thinking about the whole thing, it occurred to me that something must have given him the impression that you and I were going out together … or maybe someone did. Did you tell them anything that I'm not aware of?"

"I did not." He answered quietly and firmly. This talk was getting him upset.

"Well, I told him there's nothing between us."

"Did he want a relationship with you?"

"Well, he didn't say it, which was a good thing. I wouldn't be interested and I wouldn't want our friendship to be strained."

Sam didn't talk.

She went on, "How could I be in a relationship with a student?"

"What if God says so?"

"If it's God, I will accept it but of course, God must have spoken to me and convinced me about it."

"How will you know it's God?"

She glanced sideways at him as if she thought that was a stupid question. "Of course I will know. He talks to me, I'm His child. He will guide me. I'm not like some ladies who don't know their right from left, who don't know how to hear from God, and end up making avoidable mistakes. God will have to be involved."

Sam took a breath. He would have to add that to his prayer points.

"I can't just accept the words of a man with a sweet mouth. Besides, Sylvester is not my type."

"Who is your type?"

She laughed. "Wait till then. You will see him."

He forced himself to smile as he asked, "I don't understand that statement. Is there someone?"

She laughed again and shrugged.

Some minutes after, she entered her car and lowered the window. Sam stepped away as she started the car.

"We'll talk later." He said and waved.

"Bye." She waved back and pulled out.

In his room, he prayed that God would talk to her and convince her if she was the right person for him. Ann was spiritually strong. She wasn't the type that could be cajoled by mere words.

The following Sunday, after service, Ann told Sam she would be going with three other people to Kenya for a three-week course.

Travelling for three weeks?

"We are leaving in two weeks." She added.

"Is it certain?"

"Yes."

"Who are the other people?"

"Dora, Audu and Odein. Odein is the one I said gave me a set of shoe and bag for my birthday." Then she added, "I hope he won't see this trip as an opportunity to say any rubbish to me."

"What do you mean?"

She smiled. "Recently, he's been coming to my office." She shook her head. "He talks too much."

That latter part did not interest him. "What's he coming to do?"

She shrugged. "Talk. It seems he's showing some kind of interest though.'

"In you?"

"Yes."

He sighed.

He had to say something, so he forced a smile and said, "Oh, wow! We'll miss you."

"Who are the 'we'?" She asked.

"All of us." He answered. Then added, "Including me."

She laughed. "That's good to know. I'll miss all of you too."

"Try and get a church to attend when you get there, if it's possible."

"I will."

She left.

♥ Chapter 10

In his room, Sam got in bed and stared at the ceiling. He began to think and pray. She would be away for three weeks. Should he wait for her to come back before telling her his mind? He wasn't sure. What if another man had wooed her by then?

By 6pm, he had reached a decision. He couldn't wait any longer, he had to tell her tonight.

He took his cell phone and called her. "Where are you?"

"I'm at home."

"I need to see you about something. Can I come over right away?"

"You want to come this evening?"

"I don't mind."

"I hope there's no problem."

"No, there's none."

"Okay, you can come."

"I won't want to come inside the house though. Can we meet outside?"

"No. Really, I prefer to have whoever wants to see me come in. It's safer that way."

"You're right. It's just that I don't feel comfortable coming into the living room."

"I've told you it doesn't matter."

"I know ... can we stay at the balcony?"

"Yes."

"Okay. I will be there soon." He said.

At about 7.30pm, he was there and they went to the balcony.

"How are you?" He asked, sitting down.

"I'm alright." She said. "Would you like something to drink?"

"No."

She sat and looked at him, waiting to hear what he had to say. She noticed that he looked a little uneasy.

"The weather is cool this night."

Smiling, she said, "It is but I'm sure you didn't come all the way to tell me that. What is it you wanted to see me about, that couldn't wait? I hope everything is okay?"

He swallowed hard. He was happy they had come out to the balcony. It was dark and she would not be able to see the expression on his face.

"Er ... I want to tell you something and ... I want you to please listen and let me finish before you say anything."

"Okay. You look very serious." Ann said.

He spoke again, "Also ... in case you don't like what I'm about to say, please don't let it affect our friendship, because that matters a lot to me."

She nodded, still looking at him.

"One other thing, I will want you to pray about the matter before you make any decision."

I hope it's not what I think it is, Ann thought.

"What is it, Sam?" She was surprised that someone who seemed to have answers to every question seemed to be nervous and at a loss for words. The issue must be serious then.

Taking a deep breath, he plunged in. "I'll start from the beginning. In July last year, I came to pick you at the airport. The next day, I drove you back to the airport to pick Daniel. That day, you became a Christian and to my greatest surprise, your conversion was genuine. You began to attend our fellowship and I regarded you as my friend. And as far as I was concerned, that was all."

Ann was still looking at him, wondering what was coming.

He went on. "Later on, I began to sense that there was something special about you. I became very fond of you and I started to pray. I don't want to use the phrase 'God said', but the truth is that I've fallen in love with you and I believe with all my heart that God is involved in this. I don't know how it happened. It was not planned and it was the last thing on my mind."

He sat back and exhaled loudly, to indicate that a great burden had been lifted off his mind.

Ann laughed a little. "I'm speechless! I don't know what to say."

"You don't have to say anything now. I just wanted you to know. I've never felt like this about any lady"

"Well, as you said earlier, I will have to pray about it, and afterwards, I'll give you my answer. Until then, let's not talk about it." She said decisively.

"That's okay by me." He quickly said. "But please, let's remain friends."

"Fine. Do you want something to drink?"

He declined with the wave of a hand. "No, I'm okay. I'll be leaving soon."

"Why? Have something to drink."

He looked at her face and tried to read her feelings. She didn't seem angry.

He decided to change his mind because he was actually thirsty. "Okay. Thanks."

She went in and soon emerged with a bottle of malt for him.

"Thanks." He said again.

He sipped a little. As he put the glass cup down, he heard her chuckle.

"What?"

She laughed as she answered, "Nothing."

He smiled, "Tell me what's on your mind. Are you angry?"

"No, I'm not angry, just surprised."

"I was surprised myself. It was the last thing on my mind and when I realized what was happening, I struggled with it. I told God No, because you see, I've always prayed to marry a virgin." He shrugged, "But well, I guess it doesn't matter. What matters is salvation. As the Bible says, if anyone is in Christ, he is a new creation. Old things have passed away and everything has become new."

Ann made a sound as she quietly said, "I am a virgin."

He looked at her sharply. "You are?"

She nodded. "Yes."

He looked doubtful. "But … how's that possible? … I mean … Daniel -"

Her lips curved into a smile. "Nothing happened between us."

He still found it difficult to believe. "But … you were in S.A together, and came to Nigeria together."

Smiling, she shook her head. "There was nothing."

"I'm sorry for asking but I find it difficult to believe that a man like Daniel would not ask for sex."

"He did of course. I was the one who didn't want it. When we were in S.A, I declined having sex with him because I felt he was not committed to me, and afterward,

I came to Nigeria and became a Christian, and I told him an outright No."

He laughed. "Wow! This is interesting!"

"It is. Are you one?" She returned his question.

He laughed again. "Yes, I am."

"That makes it very interesting. It's hard to find a guy who has never done it, a guy who is pure and has the fear of God. Quite a number of people don't have the fear of God, including some people who claim to be Christians."

Sam laughed again.

She went on. "But of course, you know that the fact that you asked for a virgin and I happen to be one does not mean that's a confirmation that I'm the right lady for you."

He nodded immediately. "Of course, I know that." *Wow! This lady understands how spiritual things work.*

"I know you know that, so don't put any pressure on me. And as I said earlier, I don't want to discuss it again. I'll let you know when I have an answer for you."

He nodded and said, "I understand. And as I said earlier, let's remain friends."

In his heart, he was sure he had found his wife. He would have to pray that God would speak with her as she had said they should not discuss it again. That was one more prayer point.

He asked her about her trip.

On his way back to the campus, he began to pray. *God, talk to her. I don't want to lose her.*

****

Mid-day on Monday, Odein strolled into Ann's office and greeted her and James. He sat on the edge of Ann's table, swinging one leg, as he talked.

"I'm sure you would have bought a lot of things in preparation for the trip." Odein said.

"What things? What's there to buy?" Ann asked.

"Things like shoes and bags, clothes -"

"Why should I buy them just because I'm going to Kenya for training? What's wrong with the ones I have?" Ann asked with raised eyebrows.

He looked surprised at her answer. "You are travelling! Aren't you supposed to shop specially for it? Is that not what a typical lady would do?"

He looked at James. "Isn't that what your wife would do?"

James shook his head. "I'm not sure of what my wife would do. In recent times, I don't seem to understand her anymore. She seems to have changed."

They laughed.

"That's how women are, including those who are Christians." Odein said.

"Has it ever occurred to you that there's a reason for everything a woman does?" Ann asked Odein.

"And has it ever occurred to women that men have reasons for what they do?" Odein asked.

Then he began to talk about two of his friends who were having extra marital affairs and how he was sure their wives pushed them into it.

Ann and James tried to tell him that extra marital affair is not the solution to marital problems but he insisted he was right.

"Believe me, some women change after marriage." He declared. "My married friends discuss with me." Then he smiled and told Ann, "I hope you won't change after marriage."

"That's between me and the man I marry." She answered.

"Are you in a relationship?"

"That's a personal question." She told him.

"I need a good lady to marry." He revealed.

Then he laughed and began to tell them of the pressure his mother had been giving him to get married. When he eventually stopped, he asked Ann to go with him for lunch.

She shook her head and gave him an excuse.

"Why? I won't bite you ... And besides, I'm paying. Is there any lady who doesn't like free lunch?"

"Well, you've just met one." Ann told him.

Feeling insulted, Odein left.

Ann exclaimed, "Did he really expect me to go to lunch with him after all the rubbish he said?"

James laughed.

****

Sam did not hear from Ann. It was now three days since he told her he loved her. He would have called her but didn't want her to think he was putting pressure on her. Why had she not been in touch with him? He hoped he had not made a mistake by expressing his love.

But when by Thursday, he still hadn't received a text or call from her, he sent a text message to her, to know if she was alright. She replied and said yes.

Half-afraid she might not be in church on Sunday, he sent another text message to her on Saturday.

On Sunday, she was in church again to Sam's great relief. After service, she told him she had to leave immediately as she needed to go to the salon to fix her hair and get some things done.

"When exactly are you travelling?"

"We are leaving on Thursday."

"Do you have the flight details?"

"Not yet. We will get them tomorrow, including the tickets."

On Monday evening, when he called her, he asked about her ticket confirmation and she said she had them already.

"Which airline?"

"Kenyan Airline."

"What time are you supposed to be at the airport?"

"We should be there by 9am."

"Oh, okay."

On Thursday, while Ann and the others were on the queue to be checked in at the airport, she heard someone say hello from behind her.

She turned and saw Sam. Surprised, she glanced around, expecting to see some people with him but there was none.

"What are you doing here?"

"I've come to see you off."

"Didn't you go to work today?"

"I got permission from my boss."

Ann stepped away from the others so she could talk with him. "You didn't tell me you would be coming."

"I didn't plan to. It was a last minute decision. It occurred to me that I've not prayed with you."

She smiled. "You shouldn't have bothered."

"I know. I wanted to." He looked down at her luggage. "Is everything okay?"

"Yes."

"Let's pray."

He prayed briefly. Then looking in the direction of her colleagues, he asked, "Who is Odein between the two men?"

Ann laughed. "The taller one."

Sam fixed his gaze on the good looking man who wore jeans and shirt, and gesticulated as he talked with Dora and Audu.

"Why did you want to know?" She asked him.

He shrugged. "I just asked."

She smiled. "Are you jealous?"

He shrugged again. "Maybe."

She laughed. "Relax and pray. Expect God's will to be done."

He smiled. Glancing at his watch he said, "I have to leave. Have a safe journey."

****

On the plane, Odein came to where Ann and Dora sat and began to talk.

Ann told herself she would have to stay close to Dora and avoid Odein during this trip. She also prayed that God would make him lose interest in her.

Soon, the plane landed at Jomo Kenyatta Airport. Mr. Munyuko, a fair, tall and balding man from Thomas Lois International Training Centre was on hand to receive them. He led them outside to an eight-passenger van. A man who appeared to be in his late thirties came down from the van and greeted them.

"This is Eric. He will be your driver for the three weeks." Mr. Munyuko said.

Eric loaded their suitcases into the boot of the vehicle and drove them to a Guest House where four rooms had been booked for them.

Ann liked her room which was on the first floor. She entered the adjoining bathroom and found it was equally good. She had a shower, changed her clothes and went to join the others at the restaurant which was attached to the Guest House.

While they ate, they talked and asked Mr. Munyuko many questions. He told them the major languages Kenyans speak: English and Swahili.

Audu said he would need a cell phone as he would want to call his family. They all wanted cell phones and the man promised to get phones for them.

After making sure they were comfortable, Mr. Munyuko left with the driver to make arrangements for the phones. Half an hour later, he came back with the phones.

When Ann returned to her room, she called her parents, and Mr. and Mrs. Noah. She sent text messages to Sam and Pastor Emma so they would have her phone number.

Ann noticed that there was no fan or air-conditioner in the room, yet it was very cold.

In the night, she found herself praying again, her mind spinning. *God, You need to talk to me so I can do Your will. Is it Sam, or Pastor Emma?*

She began to think about Pastor Emma, asking herself questions. *What do I know about him?* He was a Christian and a pastor. He had a good job and wanted to marry her but ... somehow, she didn't feel she really knew him well enough. They had met and talked a number of times but she didn't feel close or free with him. If she married him, would she be free to be herself? Would he respect her personal freedom? Would he not be a controlling type? And though he had apologized for the way he treated her the other day, what was the assurance that it would not happen again?

Hmm. She rolled over to her side.

What about Sam? She began to think of him. He was good, considerate and kind. He had surprised her by coming to the airport to see her off. He was a Christian and planned to become a pastor. She liked him as a person and felt he would make a good husband.

She asked herself another question. Does he manifest the fruits of the Spirit such as gentleness, kindness, love and self control? She felt he did. Was he a violent person? The answer came to her immediately, No. Then he seemed to qualify.

But could she marry him? Another issue to consider was that he had nothing. He was just coming up in life and came from a very humble background.

That shouldn't matter though, or should it? Hmm. She sighed.

Or could the right person be Odein? She asked herself. Though she had written him off in her heart, she realized she hadn't asked God for His opinion on the matter.

"Lord, if it's Odein, I'm willing to change my mind. All I want is Your will, to please You."

As she prayed and thought about Odein, her mind told her it couldn't be him. He was not a deep Christian and would bore her in no time at all. She couldn't have a good marriage with him and as such, shouldn't marry him.

She continued praying, *Lord, make me know what to do, reveal who they are to me. Help me make the right decision.*

The next day, after breakfast, Eric drove them to the Training Centre. When he was leaving, Odein told him to come back at 4pm to pick them.

At 4pm, Eric was back to pick them and they left.

"Do you want to go back to the Guest House or would you like to see some places?"

"Ladies, what do you think?" Odein asked, turning to Ann. "Let's go out."

They all agreed to go out.

As Eric drove on, he pointed out places of interest. When they were passing through Kawangware, he told them to wind up their windows.

"Why?" Dora asked.

"Er, this area is very rough. Ladies especially have to be careful here. Some hoodlums could put their hands in the car and pick your handbags or cell phone. "

They returned to the Guest House at about 7pm.

While they were having dinner, Ann's phone began to ring. She checked and saw Sam's number. She picked it and they talked briefly.

On Saturday, Eric drove them first to Karen Nakumatt Shopping Mall where they bought some things. From there, they went to Kilimani. Eric showed them some beautiful houses and bookshops where they bought books.

On Sunday, Eric came back and drove them to a church on Lenana road.

The following Saturday, Eric arrived to take them out.

"Eric, how do I say 'How are you?' in Swahili?"

"*Habari yako.*"

Then pointing at him, she said, "*Habari yako.*"

Eric laughed and said, "*Mzuri.*"

"What's that?"

"Fine." He answered.

"Okay. What is 'come'?" Ann asked.

"*Kuja.*"

She repeated it.

"Where are we going today?" Audu asked Eric.

"I'll take you to The Giraffe Centre and Kazuri Beads and Pottery."

They reached The Giraffe Centre and after paying toll at the gate, they entered. There were many visitors there, mostly Whites. It was Ann's and Dora's first time of seeing a giraffe.

The giraffes were kept in a field by a fence. There was a wooden building on a side, and visitors stood at its balcony to feed the giraffes.

"Would you like to feed them?" Eric asked them.

"Yes. Let's go." Audu said.

They went to the balcony.

"Hey, look at that!" Dora said.

They looked in the direction of her gaze and saw a white lady kissing one of the giraffes.

Dora twisted her face in irritation.

Odein was the first to feed a giraffe. He gave his camera to Audu who took his pictures. All of them did the same and then came down the stairs.

"You will wash your hands here." Eric told them, pointing at a place.

They went there and washed their hands.

They saw some tortoises in an enclosure and went there. They also took some pictures.

They eventually left and went to Kazuri Beads and Pottery where they saw assorted hand-made, hand-painted beads.

"Wow! They are nice!" Dora and Ann exclaimed.

"My wife will love them." Audu said.

Smiling, Eric said, "Kazuri means small and beautiful."

"The beads are beautiful." Ann said.

They bought some of them.

When they were leaving, the sales manager told them, "*Asante sana.*"

"What does that mean?" Dora asked.

"That is thank you." The man said and laughed.

The following weekend, Eric took them to Nairobi National Park. From there, they went to Nairobi National Museum where they saw snakes, crocodiles and turtles, among other things.

On their way back, Dora asked Eric if he was married.

He said yes and told her about his wife.

"Where are your parents?"

He told her.

"How many siblings do you have?"

"I had six: three brothers and three sisters but two of my sisters died last year as a result of AIDS."

"Two of them?" Ann asked.

They all began to talk about the scourge of AIDS.

On Thursday, which was their last day in Kenya, they returned to the Guest House early and began to prepare for their return.

Sam called Ann at about 4pm, being the sixth time he would call her since she got to Kenya. Pastor Emma had called her twice.

She told Sam that she and her colleagues would leave the next morning for Nigeria.

****

Back in Nigeria, one of the drivers of First Place Investment Company was at the airport to pick them. They put their suitcases in the small bus he brought and left. Odein was the first to be dropped off.

Ann called her parents, Mr. and Mrs. Noah, and Sam, to inform them she was back.

On Saturday at about 5pm, Mrs. Noah knocked the door of her room and announced that Pastor Emma was in the living room to see her. Ann went to meet him. After giving him soft drink, she gave him the T-shirt she brought from Kenya for him.

As they were talking, they heard voices and soon, the front door opened and Olu entered, followed by Sam.

Sam was smiling and wanted to say something witty to Ann but when he saw that she was not alone, he said a simple 'Good evening'.

Ann introduced him to Pastor Emma. "This is Sam."

Oh, the Pastor Emma, Sam thought, greeting the man. Then he sat down.

"Let me get you something to drink." She said and got up.

She returned, served him and sat down.

As Sam sipped, he asked how she was.

He stole a glance at Pastor Emma and saw that he looked angry. He smiled.

When he finished his drink, he got up to leave and Ann saw him to the door.

"I'll call you later." He told her.

Ann closed the door and turned to walk back to her seat but saw Pastor Emma suddenly get up and stand in the middle of the room.

Ann stopped.

"Come here!" He commanded her.

"No!"

"I said come here!"

"No! You shouldn't talk to me like that!"

He walked toward her and said, "I'll talk to you the way I like!"

He pushed her back and she fell on the sofa. "Who was that man?"

"If you touch me again, I'll call my uncle!" Ann told him.

"Who was that? Was that the man you visited when you did not come home the other time?"

Ann didn't talk.

"I asked you a question!"

The balcony door opened and Pastor Emma moved away from Ann, going back to sit. Mrs. Noah entered and walked toward the kitchen. Ann got up and went to stand close to the door leading to the balcony where her uncle was.

"Pastor Emma, I don't think we are compatible. Maybe you should leave now." She said.

"Ann, it's not an issue of compatibility. It's an issue of behavior. This is the second time you would do something wrong. We are not yet married and you're making me doubt you."

"Pastor Emma, I haven't done anything wrong! I'm a Christian, I'm not wayward. I haven't done anything that would make you doubt me. The other time you referred to, if I had told you what happened to me, why I couldn't come home, would you have believed me?"

"Ann -"

"No! I doubt you would. And if you must know, just as you said you would want to marry me, Sam also proposed to me. What I told you was what I told him, that I would pray about it. I haven't cheated on you because there's no relationship yet. I'm surprised you're pushing and threatening me already."

He calmed down. "I'm sorry."

"You have anger problem, Emma. I think you should handle that first before talking about marriage."

He looked a little shame-faced. "I'm dealing with it. You can be sure it won't happen again."

"So you said the other time."

"Ann, I'm not crazy, I'm a Christian. I don't just lose my temper. Something triggers it off. I want commitment. You won't see my temper again if you don't give me any reason to doubt you." He told her.

Ann was shaking her head.

"Don't shake your head, Ann. What we need to do is try to understand each other better, to know each other's likes and dislikes. Try to understand me and there won't be any problem again." Pastor Emma continued.

"Alright, I'll think about it. But let me ask you a question, was there any time you hit your former fiancée?"

He cut her off. "That's not relevant to our discussion."

"It is. You said we should try to know each other's likes and dislikes. I'm trying to know more about you so I can avoid things that could upset you." She explained.

"Well, maybe it happened once. She knew the things I didn't like but kept on doing them."

She had her answer. He hit the lady. Noted.

When he eventually left, Ann called Mrs. Noah.

"I need to discuss something with you." Ann said.

Mrs. Noah came to the living room and they sat together.

"It's about Pastor Emma. He has anger problem." Ann said and told her how he treated her today and about the first time it happened.

"What should I do?"

"Well, I won't tell you what to do but I'll tell you this, men who hit their wives don't usually change. The reason they don't change is because they see the other person as the one at fault. They say they are provoked and make excuses for their behavior."

Ann nodded. "That's what happened. He said I caused him to lose his temper. He said the same thing about his former fiancée."

She told Mrs. Noah what Pastor Emma told her about the fiancée.

"When I asked him if he hit her at anytime, he said he did once."

Mrs. Noah snorted. "My guess is it happened more than once. The day he said he would slap you, do you think if your uncle hadn't been around or if it had happened in his house, he wouldn't have carried it out?"

Ann sighed.

"Had it been somewhere else, he would have done it! That's the truth! If he's treating you like this now, how do you think he would treat you in marriage? A man who does not respect you in public, you can imagine how he would treat you behind closed doors."

Ann nodded.

"A man who threatens to slap a lady will definitely whip her in marriage."

"So, maybe I should tell him to stop coming?" Ann wanted to know.

"The question is, what kind of marriage do you want or what kind of a man do you want? A man who will cherish you or one who will maltreat you?"

Ann smiled.

Mrs. Noah went on. "Since I married your uncle twenty seven years ago, he has never hit me. One of my friends was in an abusive relationship. The first time her husband hit her, he apologized and promised to change but he did not. Soon, it happened again and again."

Ann smiled, "But it seems Uncle likes Pastor Emma. He -"

Mrs. Noah cut in. "This has nothing to do with your uncle. He's not the one who will live with Pastor Emma. Besides, I'm sure your uncle would tell you to leave Pastor Emma if he should hear all you have told me."

Ann nodded. "That's true. Thank you, Aunty."

Soon after in her room, Ann called Pastor Emma and told him she could not marry him.

He tried to tell her that she was making a mistake but she told him her mind was made up.

"I'll see you in the office." He said.

"Don't bother to see me please."

After the call, she lay in bed, thinking. Pastor Emma was out of the picture now. It remained only Sam. *Sam? Is he the one? Let me know who he is, Lord.*

She continued to think of him. He was good for her. He looked good and had a good character. He was the kind of man she would want to marry but ... he was just up-coming and had nothing, was she ready to manage with him?

She would not want a situation where she would say 'Yes, I'll marry you', and afterward change her mind and say 'No'.

She continued praying, searching her heart. Then she decided to call Mrs. Afe and ask for her opinion on the matter.

"I understand your concerns." Mrs. Afe said quietly. "Your concerns about finance and his status are legitimate, they make sense, but then, should they guide your choice of a partner? Are they the most important things to consider? The answer is no. You may wonder why. It's simply because God can change them in the twinkling of an eye."

"Yes."

Mrs. Afe went on. "He can make a servant sit on the throne and He can bring a king down from the throne, He has the whole world in His hands. When a man's ways please the Lord, He will elevate and transform his life."

"That's true." Ann said.

"Sam may not look like what you're looking for now, but that doesn't mean he's not the real thing. Don't bother so much about where he is now, it's where he's going that matters. If he's as nice as you have told me, and he truly loves you, then everything will be alright."

"Wow! Thank you. I'm glad I called you. My regards to your husband." Ann told the woman, feeling greatly relieved.

She now had her answer.

There remained only one thing. She prayed, *Lord, I will need to be head over heels in love with Sam, the kind of love that will make me submit and stand by him to the end. If it's him, fill my heart with love for him.*

The next day after service, as Sam made his way toward Ann, she looked at him and thought, *This is my husband. He's not bad looking.*

She told Sam she brought some things from Kenya for him.

"I need to see you privately. Can we go somewhere to talk?" He said.

"Alright."

As he drove out of the compound of the University, she looked at him. Somehow, she felt like she was going on a date with him. She was surprised she was now thinking of him as a man, and not a church member anymore.

They drove to a small restaurant and ordered snacks and soft drinks.

"I missed you." Sam said, looking into her eyes.

Ann smiled, suddenly feeling shy.

His eyes went to her lips and he suddenly had a strong urge to hold her in his arms and kiss her. *No, I can't do that*, he lectured himself. That would complicate issues.

"Did you miss me?" He asked.

"Umm, I guess."

"You guess?" He kept his gaze on her, trying to gauge her feelings. Did she feel anything for him?

He asked about her trip, wanting to hear the details, which she gave.

Then he asked, "How involved are you with Pastor Emma? What happened after I left yesterday?"

She laughed. "He was very angry."

He joined in her laughter. "I knew it. He looked angry. Let me advice you, and don't think it's because I want you for myself. Don't make the mistake of marrying that man."

She laughed. "I won't see him again. I've already told him I can't marry him."

"That means you haven't told me all that happened yesterday."

Smiling, she told him how Pastor Emma pushed her and she fell on the sofa, adding that it wasn't his first time of pushing her. She explained everything to him.

"He pushed you?" Sam found it difficult to believe. "Well, I'm glad he's out of the picture. You will also need to be careful with him at the office or when you go for fellowship."

"I will."

They continued talking.

Then he asked, "I'm certain you have been praying about what I told you. Do you have an answer for me?"

Should I tell him now? She asked herself. Not yet. She decided to study him a little more.

Smiling, she said, "I thought I told you not to discuss it with me until I'm ready."

"I'm a man, Ann. A man pursues. I need to know if you have an answer for me."

Still smiling, she said, "Well, I'm still praying."

"Don't make me wait for too long."

"We'll see about that. Your birthday is in three weeks. Any plan to celebrate it? You'll be twenty five years old."

He shook his head. "I don't plan to do anything. If you're free to go out with me, we can just have lunch or dinner together, that's all."

In the car, she gave him the things she brought from Kenya for him: two T-shirts, one book, and a tie. She gave him a T-shirt for Ade and a set of beads for Mummie.

 **Chapter 11**

On the 26th of March, which was Sam's birthday, Ann sent a text to him in the morning.

Happy birthday, Sam. I'll pick u up at 5.30pm for dinner. Expect me.

About a couple of minutes after, she got a reply from him.

Tanx. Will expect u. Dinner is on me.

She sent another message.

It's on me. It's my gift to u.

He replied.

Ok. Tanx. See u at 5.30pm.

Ann wore a blue cotton blouse on white trousers, and left for Sam's campus, getting there at 5.42pm. Sam wore a black dinner jacket on a white shirt and black trousers. He entered the car and they went to a restaurant. The large room which was dimly lit had a high ceiling. A waitress in white and red uniform appeared and led them to a table for two and they sat down. She gave them two plastic-coated menus.

Looking at them, they chose cream of chicken soup as appetizer, and chicken and chips special as the main dish.

Soon, the lady returned with the soup.

As Ann and Sam took it, they talked lightly.

Then Ann put her spoon down and called him. "Sam," "Umm?"

With a sparkle in her eyes she said, "Tell me why I should marry you."

He laughed and put his spoon down. "Wow! That's a big question."

She laughed and swung one leg over the other.

Though he wasn't expecting the question, he leaned forward and began to talk.

"You should marry me because I truly and sincerely love you. I will take care of you, protect you, nourish you, cherish you and honor you. I will always be there for you no matter what happens. I won't abandon you."

Ann concentrated on him, considering and weighing his words.

He went on. "You should marry me because I am your friend and I'll always be your friend. I will be a good husband as well, and a great lover to you."

She chuckled. "Really?"

He smiled. "Don't doubt it. Everything I'm telling you is the truth. Give me the chance to prove it."

"That's good."

He continued. "You should marry me because you would be happy with me. I know you have a ministry. If you marry me, you would have the opportunity to fulfill it. With me, you would be free and able to fulfill your purpose in life. I would support you with all I have. I would not cheat on you, for me there would be no other

woman. I would never lift my hands up to hit you. I will -
"

Ann raised a hand to stop him. "That's enough."
Sam laughed.
"One more question." She said. "How do you intend to take care of your family since you said you're going to be a pastor and have a church?"
"That's simple. I will continue to work while I run the church. I will do all that I need to do to support my family. You know I'm not lazy. My family will not suffer. I know someone like you would want a man who would be able to provide her with the comforts of life but trust me, I will provide them for you, with time."
She smiled, took her spoon and continued taking her soup.
Sam spoke again. "I'm sure I've been able to convince you that I'm the right man for you."
She smiled. "You seem very sure of yourself."
"I am. Have I been able to convince you that I'm the right man for you?" He asked again. He needed to know the answer.
"Yes." She said, still smiling.
He was surprised. "I have?"
She nodded.
"So?" Did he dare hope she would agree to marry him?
"I will marry you."
"Yes!" He threw a hand up in victory.
Ann laughed.
"Thank you, Ann! You won't regret this, I promise you." He said. "Wow! This is the best part of your gift to me."

The waitress brought the main meal which was chicken and chips special. They finished the soup, pushed the bowls aside and began to eat the meal.

Ann asked another question. "Is there something I need to know about you?"

"Like what?" He asked with raised eyebrows.

"Something about you, about your past and life that would matter to our relationship." She said.

"Like a child or wife somewhere, or a criminal record or something?" He asked with a smile, then shook his head. "No. I think you already know all the important things."

He stopped for a few seconds then spoke again. "You've seen photographs of my family. You know I come from a very humble background." He shrugged. "If I had a say in the matter when I was being born, I would probably choose rich parents but I didn't have a say, I wasn't consulted." He smiled.

He continued, "I don't have regrets though. I have a wonderful family and I love them very much."

"That's good. Money is not an issue for me."

"Maybe I should ask you a similar question." He said.

She smiled. "I think you know all the important things. Of course, you know I don't have a child since I've never been involved in the act that could produce one."

He smiled. "Any allergy?"

She shook her head. "None that I know of."

They finished the food and had fruit platter as dessert.

Ann paid the bill and they left the restaurant, walking hand in hand to the car. He opened the door for her and waited for her to enter. When she did, he closed the door and moved round to the driver's side and entered.

He turned to her and said, "Now that we have agreed to get married, we have to be honest and as open as possible with each other."

She nodded in agreement.

Placing his right hand at the back of her seat, he spoke again, "Something has been on my mind. It's in the past and I don't doubt all you told me about it but I'd like to know what really happened the day you went to see Daniel and couldn't leave."

She told him in detail all that happened.

He smiled. "I'm glad God kept you."

"God apparently had a plan for me all along and somehow, kept me back from messing around. He obviously was preparing me for my future. I believe He brought us together for a purpose."

"I believe so too." He said.

Taking her hand, he leaned forward a little.

The look in his eyes told her he was struggling with his emotions. Was he going to kiss her? She could feel her heart fluttering.

He moved back and dropped her hand. Fastening his seatbelt, he put the key in the ignition and turned it. The engine roared to life.

On the way to her house, he said, "I'd like you to meet my family soon."

"That's okay. When would you want it to be?"

"Next weekend or sometime soon?"

She thought about it. "Er, let's make it upper Saturday, that's April 9."

He agreed.

At home in bed, she thought about their outing and all that happened. She remembered the look in his eyes when he took her hand in the car. She was sure he'd wanted to kiss her. Why hadn't he? And what would she have done if he had?

She began to imagine what kissing him would be like. Suddenly realizing what she was doing, she stopped, giving herself a mental shake. Her emotions must be controlled.

****

On the Saturday, Sam and Ann met and left for his parents' house, with Sam driving.

He told her he discussed with Mrs. Payne during the week that he would want to come back to Penny Books to work after the National Service, and she agreed.

"So, I have a job waiting for me."

"That's nice." She said.

"But I hope I'd get something much better by then."

She told him she would like to begin to worship in another church as Sam would leave Livingston University soon.

"I want a church where I can join a department and function better." She added.

"It has occurred to me too. It makes sense. Do you have a particular church in mind?"

"Not really."

He suggested three churches. They discussed about them and decided she should begin to worship at Rose of Sharon Chapel.

About an hour after, they reached his parents' place.

Sam parked the car in front of the house and they got down. Locking the doors, he came to her side. With a hand lightly by her waist, they entered the self-contained apartment.

His parents and siblings were in the living room. Ann knelt down to greet his parents.

"We are pleased to meet you." They told her. "Please sit down."

She did and Sam sat beside her. Looking around the small room, she saw local mats behind the door which she was sure some of them slept on.

"Would you like to eat?" His mother asked, looking from Sam to Ann.

"No. We're not eating." Sam answered.

He called his youngest brother and gave him money to get two bottles of soft drink from across the road.

The boy left, followed by one of his brothers. Ann heard them telling someone outside that Sam had brought his wife. Finding it funny, she smiled.

The boys soon returned and while Ann and Sam sipped the drinks, Sam's parents asked Ann questions, trying to get to know her better.

Sam and Ann spent about an hour and left.

In the car, they continued talking, discussing their future.

"I don't think we should have a long courtship." Sam said. "My feelings for you are strong. I wouldn't want us to make the mistake of having sex before marriage."

"Let's discuss the issue of sex first and agree. There won't be anything like premarital sex, right?"

"Right." He answered. "That's why I said we shouldn't have a long courtship."

Ann nodded. "When would you want us to get married?"

"It depends on you. When would you want it to be?"

"Well, I've always thought of getting married at the age of twenty five or twenty six."

"It can still happen. We can get married next year."

"Yes, maybe by first or second quarter of the year."

Sam liked the idea.

She spoke again. "Are we starting a family right away or should we wait for some months?"

He glanced at her. "Would you wish to wait?"

She shook her head. "No."

"I don't see any reason why we should wait."

There was a brief silence before he spoke again. "When are we going to tell our parents about our plans? They need to be informed and carried along."

"I'll suggest we wait until after your final examinations in June." She suggested.

He agreed. "It makes sense, although I'm sure my parents can guess already that you're special. You're the first lady I would introduce to them."

He suddenly laughed and said, "I know they'll be happy if I tell them I'm getting married. Most of my uncles married late. One got married at the age of forty, another at thirty seven. I'm sure they must have been wondering if they would live to see my children. This must be good news to them."

The next day, Ann went to Rose of Sharon Chapel to worship, and indicated her desire to go through Believer's class.

****

Sam and Ann continued to see each other, learn more and get to know each other better. There were times they called each other late in the evenings.

****

Sam sat for his final examination on June 22. In the evening, he went to Ann's office. When she closed, they left together.

On the way she asked him, "When will you be going for the National Youth Service?"

"It's in August. I'll want us to inform our parents of our plans before I leave."

"I'm visiting my parents on Saturday. I'll tell them." Ann said.

"And Mr. Noah?"

"I'll inform him too."

"I may go to my parents' house that day as well." He said. "What do you think your parents' opinion would be? What if they raise objections?"

She shrugged. "That's only to be expected but I'll let them know it's what I want to do. You're the man I want to marry. I know what I'm doing. They may frown a little but I'm sure they will agree. They want the best for me."

He gave her a sideway glance. "Why would they frown?"

"Well, they would want to consider your status, what you have and don't have. Besides, I told them about Daniel when I returned. So, I'm sure they would want to know why I left Daniel."

Sam sighed. "What will you tell them if they ask about Daniel?"

"I will tell them Daniel and I are not compatible. You're the one I want to marry."

****

On Saturday morning, Ann went to Mr. Noah in the living room.

"Uncle, Sam and I have agreed to marry each other."

He lowered the newspaper in his hand and peered at her through his glasses. "Sam? No. Why should you agree to such a thing?"

Ann smiled. "He's the one I want to marry."

"How could you say he's the one you want to marry? Is there no other man?"

"What is wrong with Sam?" She asked patiently.

Mrs. Noah emerged from the bedroom and sat with them.

Mr. Noah turned to his wife and explained, "She said she wants to marry Sam."

She smiled at Ann. "Congratulations."

He frowned at his wife. "What are you talking about? How could she agree to marry him?"

"What's bad in it?" Mrs. Noah asked with a frown. "Let her marry him if she loves him."

"A person should aim higher, not lower." He explained.

"That's what I'm doing by planning to marry him." Ann said.

"That's not what you are doing. You're bringing yourself down. Money matters in this life."

"I'm a Christian and the will of God is what matters to me, not money. Money cannot buy happiness. Besides, I love him." Ann told him.

"The fact that you are a Christian doesn't mean you should close your eyes and be foolish. All the things you're enjoying, don't you know that money bought them? You got the job you're doing through someone's influence. How can you say money doesn't matter?" He stared at her.

He went on. "Why would you marry just anybody? Have you told your parents?"

"I'm going to see them today. I will tell them." She answered.

He shrugged and hissed.

Mrs. Noah spoke. "If she loves him, you should allow her to marry him."

"Stop saying that!" He snapped at his wife. "How can she marry him? What does he have?"

Mrs. Noah smiled and said, "I'm sorry but I seem to remember that you were not a Managing Director when we got married, neither did you have a car."

He obviously didn't like his wife's statement and said, "Yes but I wasn't at Sam's level."

"He can still make it." His wife pointed out.

"I haven't said he will not make it. What I'm saying is that she should look for someone else." He said, then added, "And please, stop encouraging Ann."

Ann spoke, "She doesn't have to encourage me, Uncle. I have already decided to marry Sam. You need to believe that I know what I'm doing."

He shrugged.

In her room, Ann called Sam. "Where are you?"

"I'm almost at your house. I should be there in about ten minutes."

Ann left and entered her car. She met Sam by the gate of the house and he entered.

"Is everything alright?" He asked.

"I've told my uncle."

"What did he say?"

"He doesn't seem to like the idea."

"Why?"

She didn't talk.

"What did he say?"

"He asked me to look for someone else."

He was angry. "How could your uncle say that? He, of all people!"

"Don't worry. I told him you're the one I want to marry."

They continued talking. About an hour and a half later, they reached the house of Ann's parents.

"We'll meet later." Sam told her as he got down from the car.

"Alright."

He left while Ann entered the house.

Her parents were obviously happy to see her. She told them she would like to have a discussion with them.

"I just want to inform you that Sam and I have decided to marry each other."

"Who is Sam?" Her father asked with a frown, and looked at her mother for explanation.

"Sam is the boy who brought her here sometime ago. He's Layi's driver."

"He's no longer his driver. He's now a graduate." Ann said.

Mr. Sankey ignored what Ann said and looked at her mother. "Layi's driver? That boy?"

"Yes." Mrs. Sankey nodded.

Mr. Sankey looked at Ann. "Why do you want to marry a driver?"

Taking a controlling breath, Ann explained again. "He's not a driver, he's a university graduate, and we love each other."

"That's utter rubbish! How could you agree to marry him? How did you come about that silly idea?"

"What's wrong with the idea, Dad? Why did you call it 'silly'?"

"A lot is wrong with it! Why that boy?" He asked and then turned to his wife, pointing an accusing finger at her. "She told you all these things and you agreed!"

"I didn't agree! I'm hearing it for the first time!" Mrs. Sankey said.

"Well, you can't marry him." He said with finality.

"Dad, I love him!" Ann said.

"Keep quiet! What do you know about love?"

The corners of her mouth turned up in a smile. "I'm almost twenty five years old and you're asking me what I know about love?"

"Okay. Tell me about this Sam." Her father demanded.

"As I said, he's now a graduate. He wants to become a pastor and will work to support his family. We are planning to get married next year."

"That's definitely not going to happen!"

"Dad! Try and understand!" Ann said.

"Alright. When he gets a good job, come back and we'll talk."

"Dad!"

Her mother spoke. "What about Daniel?"

"We are not compatible."

"What do you mean by that? He's a good boy."

Ann smiled a little. "You don't know him. Believe me if I tell you we're not compatible."

They talked for some time. Her parents asked her to give them a week to think about it.

****

Sam told his parents that he had decided to marry Ann.

"Thank You Jesus!" His mother said with a smile, obviously happy at the news. "We knew she must be special to you when you told us you were bringing a lady home for the first time. This is good news."

Sam grinned. "We love each other and we're planning to get married next year."

"Next year? Why?" His father asked with a frown.

"Why don't you wait a little? If it were to be some other people, I would think the lady was pregnant, but I know you are a serious Christian. It can't be because she's pregnant." His mother said. "Why so soon?"

Sam smiled. "We want to do the right thing, that's why we want to get married next year. We don't want to indulge in premarital sex like some people do."

"Your plan is good but what about money? Where will we get money from?" His mother asked with concern.

Sam smiled again. "It's still next year. When the time comes, let me know whatever you need money for, I'll provide it."

****

At about 3pm, Ann left her parents' house. She called Sam to know where he was.

"I was just waiting for your call. I'll be on my way now. Where should we meet?"

She told him to stay at an agreed spot, and some minutes later, she reached the place. Sam took over the driving.

"So, how did it go?" He asked.

She told him what her parents said.

"We won't allow that to discourage us. We'll pray." He said.

"What did your parents say?" She asked.

"They only showed concern about money."

"What money?" She asked and turned to look at him.

"Money for the wedding."

"But it's next year!"

Sam laughed. "That's what I told them. I also promised to assist them financially when the time comes."

In the evening, Mr. Noah called Ann. "Have you told your parents about Sam?"

"Yes."

"And what did they say?"

"Well, they expressed concern like you did." She said.

"Ann, call Daniel. If there was a misunderstanding between you, try to resolve it. If it was because of what he did that day, I can talk to him and let him know it was wrong. I'm sure he would be more careful. He's a better choice."

Ann was shaking her head.

"What about Pastor Emma?" Mr. Noah asked.

"Ah!" Mrs. Noah laughed and said, "I wouldn't advise her to marry him. I know he's a pastor but God will forgive me."

Ann smiled.

"Why did you say that?" Mr. Noah asked his wife.

Mrs. Noah looked at Ann and their eyes met. "Tell your uncle." She said.

Ann told Mr. Noah of how Pastor Emma treated her the two times he was angry.

"Okay. What about Daniel or some other men?" Mr. Noah asked. "There should be a man somewhere! Is there no unmarried man in your office?"

Mrs. Noah laughed. "Honey, relax."

"Uncle, I appreciate your concern but I know what I'm doing. I'll be fine. Everything will be alright." Ann said.

"I hope so." He responded with a sigh.

The following Saturday, Ann went to see her parents again. After much talk, they agreed to allow her marry Sam.

"Thank you Daddy, thank you Mommy." Ann said happily.

****

On the last Saturday in July, Sam and Ann went to a beach, wearing jeans. They sat together and ate as they talked. He took her hand in his. Being near her was doing funny things to his heart.

She had a feeling he was struggling with his emotions and she wondered what would happen. She knew his feelings for her were strong. If he tried to kiss her, what would she do? She decided she would have to hold on to self control.

"I'd like to kiss you." He suddenly said in a husky voice, and without waiting, he held her head in his hands, leaned in and kissed her.

When he released her, she told him, "Sam, we need to be careful, especially you. If you're not careful, we'll get into trouble."

He agreed. "I'll be careful." Then he asked, "But how was the kiss? Was it good for you?"

They laughed.

"Hmm?" He wanted to know what she thought of it.

"Well, it wasn't bad." She laughed again.

They continued talking.

Then she said, "There are things we need to agree on, things that would make us have a good marriage."

"Alright. What are they?"

"We need to agree that if we have a misunderstanding in our marriage, we won't tell a third party. We will discuss together and resolve it between us. Do you agree?"

"You're speaking my mind. I agree." He said immediately.

Ann continued, "I mean ... why should we tell another person if the issue is about our marriage? If you offend me, I'll let you know, and if I offend you, please tell me. And when this happens, the one at fault must apologize."

"You're one hundred percent correct." He said. "But if it's getting prolonged and we need to talk to someone, it will only be our pastor or spiritual father."

Ann nodded. "We have also agreed that there won't be premarital sex. Right?"

"Right. No sex until we're married." He said. "We will avoid situations that could lead to it."

"Good." She said. "Also, we must not have a case of another man or another woman in our marriage. It's one of the things that destroy marriages. We are Christians and it shouldn't come up."

"I agree." He said easily. "That's not a problem."

"Also, we should be as honest and open as possible with each other. It's important we talk openly and honestly. I will want us to be ve-e-e-e-ry close. As close as possible."

"Yes, I agree but ... is there a reason for all these things you're saying? Did something happen?" He asked, a little afraid of what her answer would be.

She shook her head and smiled. "No. I just felt we should discuss and agree up front so we can have a solid foundation for our marriage."

"Splendid! While we're at it, I think we should have a special name we would call ourselves." Sam suggested.

"Okay. What would you suggest?"

"Names such as 'Honey' and 'Dear' are common. I'm thinking of a name like 'Baby' or 'My Baby'."

Ann laughed. "Why 'Baby' of all the names we can call ourselves? What about 'Mine'?"

He shrugged. "Well, you can choose what you'll call me and I'll call you what I want. I prefer 'Baby'."

She smiled. "Okay. I prefer 'Mine'."

"Or better still, we can combine the two, and have 'Baby Mine'."

Ann laughed. "It sounds good and unique."

"That's settled."

"Would anyone live with us when we are married?" She asked.

He shook his head immediately. "No. We won't have anybody live with us until we have a child. We will manage. When you're pregnant, I'll assist you as much as I can. Our mothers will definitely want to come around when you put to bed. I can also ask one of my siblings to come to assist you."

"Boys? What can they do?"

"They assist my mother at home. They will do whatever I ask them to do."

She shook her head. "No. If I need assistance, I'd prefer to make my own arrangement, get someone I would be comfortable with."

He shrugged. "That's fine. The house belongs to a woman anyway. But at any time you want me to invite my siblings to assist you, just let me know."

"Okay, thanks. About accommodation, my parents have another house in Lagos and one in Ibadan. I want to suggest that we ask them to allow us stay in one of the apartments, so we can use whatever money we have for other things including furniture, rather than spend our money paying for rent."

He shook his head slowly. "I'm not sure about this. I don't think I'll want to live in your parents' house. The best thing is to move away from parents, and that's scriptural."

"I know. I never planned to live in my parents' house as well but with the way things are, we may have to until we are more buoyant and you have a better job."

"Can't we raise money for accommodation?"

"First, what kind of apartment are we looking at? How many rooms?" She asked.

"A two-bedroom apartment probably."

"In which area?"

"I want a good area, for security reasons." He mentioned some areas.

"Those areas will be expensive." She mentioned an amount.

"Can we think of how to raise it?"

"It's between the two of us. How much can you get from your end?"

"Nothing. He sighed.

"Another thing we can do is postpone our wedding. The decision is ours."

He took a deep breath. "Are you certain that your parents would not object to our staying in their house?"

"If I tell them, I'm sure they will understand and agree."

He shook his head. "I don't know. I'm not sure about this. I will have to think about it carefully."

"That's okay, but I'll suggest we stay in their house. It makes sense in this case."

"It does but let me think about it." He said.

About two weeks after, Sam told her to talk to her parents about staying in their second house in Lagos, and that they would pay some token as rent to show they were responsible. If her parents agreed, good, if not, they would try to look for money and get their own apartment.

Ann discussed with her parents. Mr. And Mrs. Sankey were not too happy about the idea but agreed after much talk. They told Ann that one of the tenants in a two-bedroom flat in the house would be moving out next year, in August.

Ann was happy. "We will take it. Thank you, Daddy and Mummy."

When she saw Sam, she told him and they decided to postpone their wedding to November, the following year.

****

By the second week of August, Ann had completed the Believer's class and also Worker's class and had joined choir and prayer departments in Rose of Sharon Chapel. On the 30th of the month, Sam left for Benin, for the National Youth Service, promising to call Ann everyday until he returned. He was posted to a High School to teach Biology and Mathematics.

****

It was the 4th Monday in the month of November. Ann got back home from work and saw a black SUV in the compound.

Is ... Daniel here?

Her heart racing, she entered the house and found Daniel sitting comfortably in the living room, talking with Mrs. Noah. She was surprised. Daniel ... after ten months?

"What are you doing here?" She asked, her gaze taking in his face and dressing. He looked like a young rich man that he was.

He laughed and stood. "Is that how to greet me?"

"I'm sorry but you were the last person I expected to see." She confessed.

"I know. I wanted to spring a surprise on you."

"Well, you succeeded." She admitted.

Mrs. Noah got up and left the room.

"How are you?" She asked.

"I'm fine. And you? … although I don't think I should ask, you look good."

"Thanks. When did you come?"

"Yesterday, and I'll be leaving Monday morning."

"Wow! This is a surprise. What do I offer you?"

"Water will be fine."

"Please sit down."

She went into the kitchen to get it. She soon returned with a glass cup of water. Then she sat down.

"So, what's been happening to you?" He asked, his eyes perusing her.

She smiled. "I go to work … and ... that's it. What's happening to you?"

"I'm okay. I'm sorry I didn't get in touch with you, and I'm sorry for what happened the last time we met. I was angry at the turn of events, but you were never completely out of my mind."

She shrugged. "I've forgotten about it."

"Ann, is it too late for us to start again?"

Surprised, she asked, "Start again? Daniel?"

"Yes. Start again. I can still remember that you mentioned marriage at a time. Now, I'm ready for it."

"You? What changed your mind about marriage?"

"Life."

They laughed.

"I realize I need to settle down."

"Daniel, be honest. I'm certain there's a lady in your story somewhere."

"That's true. There was a lady." He shrugged. "It didn't work out."

"For how long were you together?"

"I met her in February and we parted ways in June."

"Why?" She asked.

"You mean why did we part ways?"

She nodded.

"It didn't work out." He flipped his hand and said, "But that's history. Let's talk about us. Ann. Let's give marriage a try. I've thought about this carefully. I will even allow you go to church, do whatever you want to do. I may go with you sometimes." He said.

He added, "I need a wife who would help me entertain my guests and who would attend functions with me."

She was tempted at the offer. Marrying him would make her parents and her uncle very happy, and also provide her some comfort. She wouldn't have to live in her parents' house and would be able to travel abroad, probably visit South Africa again soon.

But she was already in a relationship with Sam. Besides, Daniel still wasn't a Christian.

She began to shake her head.

"Don't shake your head, Ann. Please."

She shook her head again.

"Is there someone else?" He asked.

"Yes."

"Who is he? Do I know him?"

She looked away as she said, "It's Sam."

"Who? Sam? The driver?"

Why is everyone calling Sam a driver? "He is not a driver. He's a graduate."

"I should have known." Daniel said. "I told you then that you were getting too close to him but you denied it."

"It happened recently."

"But Ann, where's your sense? You could do better than that."

"Daniel, I know what I'm doing."

He snorted. "I doubt it. Ann, you could have a better life with me. I'll take care of you."

She shook her head slowly.

He told her, "I'll be at my parents' house till Monday morning. I'll expect you to get in touch. If you don't, then I'll know it's truly over and I won't get in touch with you again."

He wrote his address on a sheet of paper and gave it to her.

"Get in touch with me if you change your mind. I hope you do."

Ann saw him off.

Back in her room, she sat on her bed, troubled. Seeing Daniel again and hearing him talk about marriage and attending functions with him was the last thing she had expected. It seemed he really liked her. He still wasn't a Christian and she was supposed to hate him because of what he did to her in January but somehow, she didn't. What should she do?

She had felt Sam was the right person and had been willing to struggle with him but now, she wasn't so sure anymore. Sam was a struggling young man and would have a lot of responsibilities toward his siblings. Would she be able to cope? Was that kind of life what she wanted? Had she made a mistake by agreeing to marry him?

She cast her mind to the times she and Daniel had together in S.A. Those were good times. Suddenly, she longed to be in South Africa again.

She began to weep. How should she handle this matter? She decided to tell Sam about it, knowing she could discuss with him and he would understand. They had also promised to be honest with each other.

She took her phone and dialed.

Picking it almost immediately, he said cheerfully, "Hello Baby Mine."

"Sam, I need to discuss something with you." She told him immediately.

He felt she sounded upset and he became concerned immediately. "Are you alright?"

"Yes but -" She stopped.

"I'm listening." He encouraged.

"Daniel came. He has just left." She blurted out.

Daniel again? Sam thought, his heart racing. He felt as if he'd been knocked on the head with a hammer. "Why did he come?"

"He said he wants me back."

"Wants you back?"

"Yes."

"What's that supposed to me?"

"He said he's ready for marriage." She said, as tears began to roll down her face.

Sam heard her voice trembling and he asked, "Are you crying?"

Instead of an answer, he heard sobs.

Sobs? "Ann, why are you crying?"

"I think I still care about him ... I don't know how to handle it." She said.

Sam took a deep breath and waited for her to continue.

"He said he is leaving on Monday morning. He gave me his number and asked me to get in touch with him."

"And what did you tell him when he said that?" He asked with a frown.

"I didn't say anything."

He was very upset. "Ann, I'm surprised you didn't say anything. This is Satan's trick to confuse and distract you. You know he's not right for you, don't you?"

"I know but -"

"There's no 'but', Ann! Don't get in touch with him and don't do anything rash. I will come over immediately."

"You will come to Lagos from Benin?"

"I have to." He said.

"No, you don't have to. Just pray with me." She said.

"I will definitely pray with you but I have to come to Lagos as well. We need to talk." He said firmly.

He prayed with her before hanging up.

Ann got up and changed her clothes. Somehow, talking to Sam made her feel better.

****

After the call, Sam tossed his phone aside on the bed. He stood and began to pace the floor of his room as he prayed, asking God to intervene.

He would have to leave for Lagos early in the morning. He glanced at the wall clock. It was a little after 9pm.

Taking his phone, he called the Vice Principal of the school where he was serving, to take permission to be away for three days.

"I've just received a call from Lagos. I need to travel immediately, please." He explained.

The man easily agreed, to Sam's astonishment.

"Thank you, sir. I'm grateful." He said.

He also called two of his friends in the school to inform them that he would not be around for some days.

Afterward, he packed a small bag with the things he would need for the trip.

Early the next day, he left.

He arrived in Lagos and went straight to Ann's office. She hadn't closed and he waited at the reception. At 5pm, she joined him and they left, driving to a park where they could sit and talk. There were some adults with children there. Sam chose a quiet spot, cleaned the bench with his handkerchief and they sat down.

"Tell me all about Daniel's visit. What exactly did he say?" He asked.

As Ann talked, staring at the field, Sam searched her face closely, to know what she felt. He saw that she looked troubled.

When she stopped, he took a deep breath. "Did he tell you he still cares for you?"

She didn't answer as tears formed in her eyes. She blinked to hold them back.

He put his hand on her shoulder. "Even if he did, Ann, I need to tell you the truth, that is not the kind of love that will last. He can't love you the way you deserve to be loved, and I'm not saying this because I want you to be mine. It's what I would tell anyone I care about. A number of things are wrong with that kind of relationship, believe me. And you know it. You also know he does not believe in what you believe in. You don't have same values. The relationship would struggle until it dies. And you would eventually die unfulfilled."

She brushed a tear from her cheek and looked down.

He continued, "Besides, you and I are in a relationship. You know I love you ... and I know you love me. Maybe you feel upset and confused now but I know you love me. I will help you forget him. I love you with all my heart. I will help you, I am here for you."

He held her hand and went on. "You will soon forget him. He is not the right man for you. I will never hurt you, Ann. God brought us together. You've said it before and you know it is true. Don't get confused. What about your purpose in life? You know you have a ministry to fulfill. You can't fulfill it with him, and you know it."

He stopped and searched her face. Then he went on, "All those material things Daniel is dangling before you cannot make a marriage work. They will fail eventually. It is what our love builds that will stand the test of time. I will work hard and have money. We will have cars, we will have our own house. I will take care of you."

She was surprised at what she was hearing. She had thought he would be angry about it but he wasn't. He was indeed a good and mature man.

She stared into his eyes and saw what seemed like pain. "I'm sorry if I've hurt you by the news. I don't know what came over me."

He dropped her hand and shrugged. "It's not the kind of thing a man wants to hear. You love a lady and you're already talking about marriage but she suddenly starts crying over her ex-boyfriend. But I have to fight for you. Good things don't always come easily. We are meant to be together, I won't allow anyone or anything to take you from me. You will appreciate me more with time."

She took his hand, her lips curving into a smile. "I appreciate you now, Sam. I'm glad you're in my life. Thank you for your understanding and for being patient with me. You're a good man. I do love you."

She moved closer to him and rested her head on his shoulder, feeling comforted and strengthened. He put an arm around her shoulders and pulled her close, resting his chin on her head.

He spoke again. "Challenges will come but we must be committed to our relationship. You might meet men who might want to go out with you but you must not waver, you must close your eyes to them. I will do the same thing. We must create our own history."

She moved and he slowly released her. Taking her purse, she took the paper Daniel wrote his address on and tore it into pieces. Getting up, she walked over to where a trash bag was and threw the pieces of paper inside.

She came back to sit beside Sam and said, "I'm glad I called and told you about it."

"I'm also glad you did. If you hadn't told me, it could have become a big problem that could tear us apart. I wouldn't have known what the problem was, and wouldn't have been able to help you." Sam said. "I'm glad you found God."

Ann looked into his eyes. "And I'm glad you found me. Thank you for being patient with me."

****

From that night, Ann began to ask God to lift Sam up and bless him tremendously.

The following year, they got married on the third Saturday of November.

Also By the Same Author

In Love for Us
Love Fever
Love on the Pulpit
Shadows from The Past
This Time Around
Tears on My Pillow
Oh Baby!
To Love Again
What changed you?
Too Much Of A Good Thing
My First Love
With This Ring

30 Things Husbands Do That Hurt Their Wives
30 Things Wives Do That Hurt Their Husbands
God's Words to Singles
Devotionals for Singles
Rape & How to Handle it

And

Rescued By Victor (for children)
No One is a nobody (for children)
Greater Tomorrow (for children)
The Boy Who Stole (for children)
Joe and his stepmother, Bibi
Nike & The Stranger

About the author

Taiwo Iredele Odubiyi is a Pastor and the Executive President of TenderHearts Family Support Initiative, a Non-Governmental Organization, and Pastor Taiwo Odubiyi Ministries. She has a deep and strong passion for relationships and expresses this in ministries - nationally and internationally- to children, teenagers, singles, women and couples. She reaches out to these groups through counselling, seminars and programs such as Teenslink, Singleslink, Coupleslink, and Woman to Woman.

Married and blessed with children, she is the regular host of the TV and Radio program - It's all about you!

This is her seventh romance novel.

I love hearing from the readers of my books. If this book has blessed you, please send your comments to:

WhatsApp: +1-4108187482
Website: www.pastortaiwoodubiyi.org
Facebook: Pastor Mrs. Taiwo Odubiyi
            Pastor Taiwo Iredele Odubiyi's novels & books
Twitter: @pastortaiwoodub
Instagram: @pastortaiwoiredeleodubiyi

If you have friends and loved ones, then you do have people you should bless with copies of these very interesting and life-changing novels and books!

About the book

When Sam was helping Ann, he did not know that he was really helping himself until he fell in love with her. But what did he have to offer her? And did he have a chance when at least three other men were also interested in her?

Ann was also aware of this dilemma and she began to pray, "Lord, reveal who these men are to me!" How would she know who the right man was?

****

Learn how to know the will of God in marriage and tips on how to have a good marriage in this interesting and suspense-filled novel, YOU FOUND ME.

Printed in Great Britain
by Amazon